PEN PALS:
BOOK FOURTEEN

# THE MYSTERY
# ABOUT MAXIE

*by Sharon Dennis Wyeth*

A YEARLING BOOK

Published by
Dell Publishing
a division of
Bantam Doubleday Dell Publishing Group, Inc.
666 Fifth Avenue
New York, New York 10103

The trademark Yearling ® is registered in the U.S. Patent and
Trademark Office.
The trademark Dell ® is registered in the U.S. Patent and
Trademark Office.
ISBN: 0-440-40394-4

Illustration by Wendy Wax
Published by arrangement with Parachute Press, Inc.
Printed in the United States of America
October 1990
10  9  8  7  6  5  4  3  2  1
OPM

*For Joy and Patrick*

# CHAPTER 1

—————◆—————

Wanted: Boy Pen Pal.
Please Contact: Max Schloss, Suite 3-D, Fox Hall,
Alma Stephens School for Girls.
(P.S.: I'm a Girl!)

"I don't understand what's wrong. Your ad has been in the Ardsley *Lion* twice, Max. By now, you should be knee-deep in pen pal candidates," Amy Ho said, staring absently at the Monopoly board in front of her. Her mind was definitely not on the game the four suitemates were playing.

Three of the girls already had pen pals. They'd advertised for them under the code name "Foxes of the Third Dimension" almost exactly a year ago as freshmen at the all-girls boarding school. Boys from nearby Ardsley Academy had responded eagerly, and now only Maxie—the newest member of the suite—was without one. It was a state of affairs her friends were determined to change.

"The next time you run the ad, Max, you ought to throw in a line about your dad being a television come-

1

dian," Palmer Durand suggested. And zipping her racecar game piece around to Park Place, she added, "It wouldn't hurt a bit to let the Ardsley guys know you're related to somebody famous."

"Maxie wants a pen pal who's impressed with her, not her father. Besides, bragging about your family is tacky," Shanon Davis objected. "And so is cheating," she added, playfully tugging Palmer's wavy blond hair. "You just moved three spaces too far."

"I didn't cheat. It was an honest mistake," Palmer said, blithely backing her car up. "Anyway, it's clear that the ad needs something. Too bad the *Lion* won't run photographs in the classified section. It would definitely help if the Ardies could see how gorgeous Max is."

Maxie Schloss blushed at the unexpected compliment. Not knowing quite how to handle it, she resorted to humor—as usual. "Quick, somebody grab a camera! This pose ought to knock 'em in the aisles," she said, crossing her eyes and baring her teeth in a goofy grin.

"Quit clowning around. It's a terrific idea," Amy said. "Next time I write to John, I'll send a picture of you so he can show it around the dorm."

"And Palmer can send one to Sam so he can pin it on the bulletin board at his school, too," Shanon enthused.

Maxie raised her hands in a "time out" signal. "Hold up on the P.R. campaign, guys. The last thing I need is to have my face plastered all over beautiful downtown Brighton! Besides, the ad worked just fine. I got four more letters in the mail today."

"Four *more*?" Amy exclaimed.

"You mean there are others you haven't even mentioned?" Shanon squealed.

Maxie's flaming cheeks almost matched her red hair, and she suddenly got very interested in the pile of play money in front of her. "Sort of," she mumbled. "There were three yesterday, and six the day before—eight if you count the two postcards."

Three disbelieving gazes zeroed in on her flushed face. "Why didn't you tell us?" the suitemates protested in unison.

Maxie squirmed, answering their question with one of her own. "What's the big deal?"

Palmer plucked the Go-to-Jail card from the stack on the board and playfully flipped it into Maxie's lap. "You're breaking Suite 3-D's main rule," she teased.

"Yeah—you're one of the Foxes of the Third Dimension now, Maxie, and we always share our letters," Amy added.

"Lighten up, guys. The important thing is that she got her choice of *fifteen* pen pals," Shanon piped up. "Which one did you pick, Max?"

For once, Maxine Edith Schloss—who could talk a blue streak with hardly a pause for breath—was at a loss for words. "Well, er—I, don't—I mean—"

"Don't hold out on us, Max. Did he send you his picture?" Amy asked.

"He's probably a real hunk, and she's just afraid one of us will try to steal him away," Palmer mused aloud.

Amy slid her a sidelong glance. "And of course none of *us* would ever do a sneaky thing like that, would we, Palmer?"

Palmer, who had been guilty of that very crime more than once, flushed only slightly.

"I haven't told you about my pen pal because I have no idea who he's going to be," Maxie hastily interjected. "I haven't opened any of the letters yet." Jumping up from her spot on the floor, she retrieved a bundle of mail from her bookbag and then dropped it in the middle of the game board. "Dig in, gang."

Amy ran her fingers through her spiky black hair and let out a long whistle. "This is a major haul!"

"So what are we waiting for? On the count of three, everybody grab an envelope and rip it open," Palmer urged.

With one exception, the Foxes followed her instruction: Maxie picked up a postcard and began folding it into an airplane.

"I think we've struck pay dirt," Amy said after scanning a few lines of the note she had chosen. "This guy is an exchange student from Barcelona, Spain. His name is Alano Tarrago, and he plays tennis, soccer, and classical guitar. And get a load of the snapshot he sent!"

Almost before the words were out of her mouth, Palmer plucked the photo from Amy's hand. "I always wondered how Tom Cruise would look with curly, blond hair," she breathed, reluctantly passing the photo along to Maxie. "And just look at those eyelashes!"

"He probably has to roll them up on curlers every night," Maxie cracked, tossing Alano aside with a nervous chuckle. "A guy that good-looking is bound to be conceited."

Quick as lightning, Palmer's fingers snaked out to rescue the handsome Alano.

"Here we go again," Amy groaned. "I thought you were so crazy about your own pen pal, Palmer. Sam O'Leary is not only adorable—he's nice, too."

"It never hurts to have a spare tucked away for emergencies," Palmer said nonchalantly. "Who knows? One of these days, I might decide to take Spanish instead of French." She tucked the photo into her pocket and turned to Shanon. "Who did you get?"

"Lemuel Lawrence Langford," Shanon reported, giggling. "He's president of the chess club, treasurer of the debating team, and secretary of the bird-watcher's society. The lowest grade he ever got was a B in finger painting when he was in the first grade."

"Stick old 'triple L' back on the bottom of the pile," Palmer cast her vote. "Anyone who'd use graph paper for stationery is automatically out." She pulled a folded sheet from a square white envelope, and a smile stole over her face as she began to read:

*Dear Max,*

*Have you heard the joke about the ten-foot-tall astronaut with seven arms and three heads? No? Well, neither have I, but I'm sure it must be out of this world!*

*If you'll be my pen pal, I promise you a laugh in each letter, a howl for every hour, and I'll even throw in a snicker per second. As you can tell, I'm a side-splitting, fun-loving fool!*

*Yours very truly,*
*Ernie Kernewly*

"Kernewly and Schloss—is that a match made in heaven, or what?" Palmer said, rolling her big blue eyes to the ceiling.

"Get real. Writing to that guy would be like playing straight man in one of my dad's slapstick routines," Maxie said, sailing her postcard plane across the room with a casual snap of her wrist. She scooped up the rest of the letters from the Monopoly board and straightened the row of green houses she had bought on Baltic Avenue. "C'mon, let's finish the game."

"Forget the game. We're talking serious business here," Palmer said firmly. "Besides giving you something to look forward to at mail call, having a pen pal means automatic dates."

Shanon nodded her head in agreement. "It *is* nice to know someone at Ardsley personally."

"We're going about this all wrong," Amy said, tugging thoughtfully at the silver hexagon dangling from her earlobe. "Mixing that Lemuel character or Ernie Kernewly with the rest of the gang would be an absolute disaster. What if Maxie's pen pal doesn't get along well with all of our pen pals?"

Palmer picked up the dice and rolled them across the Monopoly board. "Wait a minute," she said enthusiastically. "Since Lisa left, Rob doesn't have anyone at Alma Stephens to write to."

Amy and Shanon stared at her in disbelief.

"No way!" Maxie was quick to object. In the few weeks since the term began, Shanon had made it clear that no one could replace Lisa McGreevy, who had been her roommate the year before. Lisa had transferred back to her local school in Pennsylvania after her parents separated so she could be with her mother. After a rocky start, Max and Shanon were getting along great, and Max was not about to do anything to jeopardize their relationship.

There was a moment of silence in which Shanon flashed her a brief smile, and then Amy piped up, "How about

Paul Grant? He's John, Rob, and Mars's new roommate."

Maxie flipped through the remaining envelopes, then shook her head. "No go. He didn't answer the ad."

"So what? I'm sure he wouldn't mind," Amy persisted. "If you and Paul started writing each other, three of the Foxes would have pen pals who are part of The Unknown," she said, referring to the boys by the name they'd used to answer the Foxes' original ad.

"Sam's *almost* an Unknown," Palmer pointed out. "After all, he was once an Ardie, and he, John, and Mars get along really well."

Maxie rolled one of the postcards into a cylinder and stuck it between her teeth like a fat cigar. "There are three unknowns in my family, too. Whoever hoid of Harpo, Chico, and Zeppo?" she said, wiggling her eyebrows. The pained expressions on her suitemates' faces told her that her Groucho Marx imitation had fallen flat. Cutting the comedy, she quickly apologized: "I didn't mean to make fun of your pen pals. Writing to boys at Ardsley is a neat idea, but I'm not really into dances and dates and stuff like that."

Palmer reached over to brush Max's forehead with mock concern. "That's got to be a fever talking," she said dramatically. "Any fourteen-year-old girl who doesn't like boys is terminally ill!"

"Wait a minute," Shanon said on Maxie's behalf. "I used to feel that way too—before I got to know Mars."

"That's right," Amy chimed in. "It's up to Max to decide who she wants for a pen pal."

Grateful for the support, Maxie smiled weakly. She wanted to fit in with her suitemates, share the invisible

7

bond that pulled Amy, Shanon, and Palmer together. But she knew that she wasn't really one of the Foxes of the Third Dimension—not quite yet.

"I *do* want a pen pal," Maxie declared. "But if I pick one by myself, I'll probably get a lemon. I really, really, really need your help." And with that, she grabbed the pile of letters and fanned them out like a deck of cards, wisecracking, "Pick one—any one at all except ol' triple L and Kernewly—and I swear I'll write him for the rest of my natural life!"

"We didn't mean to push you, Max. If you don't want to write to anyone, it's okay," Shanon told her.

Pasting on a bright smile, Maxie tossed her pen pal candidates aside with a casual, "I'll put them under my pillow tonight. Maybe the right one will come to me in a dream."

"Speaking of which, I have a real dream of an idea!" Palmer said, dumping the Monopoly game haphazardly back in its box. "I just heard that the job of Fox Hall Social Chairperson is up for grabs. Brenda Smith doesn't want it anymore."

"Too bad. We all had a great time at the pajama party she set up for the dorm last year," Amy said with a grin.

"I sure did," Palmer agreed. "I bet that was the biggest single order Figaro's Pizza ever got!"

"Mmm," Shanon recalled hungrily. "Twenty-five Monstros! But what does Brenda Smith have to do with your idea, Palmer?"

"I'm going to volunteer to take her job," Palmer proudly announced. "And the first thing I'm going to do is to set up a Fox Hall Halloween Party!"

"That might be fun," Amy said. "We could bob for apples and sit around telling ghost stories."

"You can do whatever you want to do, but I intend to spend the entire evening with Sam," Palmer said, smugly buffing her nails on the front of her sweatshirt.

Shanon gaped at her. "A party with the guys?"

"You'd better believe it," Palmer said. "Hot music, costumes, decorations—the whole bit. It'll be better than last year's Trickster Mixer."

"Palmer Durand, you're a genius," Amy squealed, dancing her roommate around the room.

Shanon joined in, and the three girls whirled until they tumbled onto the pink loveseat in a giggling heap.

The fixed grin on Maxie's face didn't waver, but she had never felt more out of it in her entire life.

# CHAPTER 2

————◆————

A knock cut short the gleeful outburst in 3-D. Before anyone could respond, Kate Majors opened the door. "How's
it going, group?" she greeted them.

Three of the Foxes chorused a bubbly "Terrific!" but
Maxie's reply was a lukewarm "Fine."

"We were celebrating a great plan Palmer just came up
with. I guess we got a little too loud," Shanon offered
guiltily.

"I didn't come to complain about the noise," the dorm
monitor said. It was easy to tell she had something more
serious on her mind. Behind her thick glasses, her eyes
were wide with concern. "Shanon, have you heard from
Lisa lately?"

"I got a note from her last week," Shanon replied with
a smile. "She said to tell you hello."

"Did she say anything about her parents' separation?"
Kate queried. "Do you think she's coping with it all right?"

Shanon gave the older girl a puzzled look. Kate had been
dating Lisa's brother, Reggie, who was an upperclassman

10

at Ardsley. She should know the McGreevy situation better than anyone.

The same thought must have occurred to Palmer, because she blurted out, "Why don't you ask Reggie?"

"He and Lisa aren't communicating much these days," Kate reported. "As a matter of fact, she seems to be shutting herself away from almost everyone. Reggie's very worried about her. He was hoping maybe she'd confided in you."

"She didn't even mention her parents the last time she wrote," Shanon said with a frown. "I just assumed everything was okay."

"Well, maybe it is," Kate said hopefully. Turning to leave the room, she added, "But next time you write, send her my best."

"Will do," Shanon agreed.

"Lisa and Reggie were always such good buddies," Amy observed as soon as Kate was out the door. "I wonder what went wrong?"

Although Maxie knew very little about the situation, she ventured a guess anyway. "Maybe she's mad because she's at home and he's still going to Ardsley."

Shanon shook her head. "You don't know Lisa," she defended. "She would never begrudge her brother the chance to stay with his class. She doesn't have a jealous bone in her body."

Maxie immediately wished she had kept her mouth shut. Not wanting to butt in where she didn't belong, she went to the desk at the other side of the room and busied herself with a pile of books she had checked out of the library.

"Max may have a point," Palmer mused aloud. "If the

McGreevys are having problems, Reggie should have transferred to a school near home, too. Why should Lisa have to make all the sacrifices? I sure wouldn't if I were in her shoes."

"Come to think of it, that doesn't seem quite fair," Shanon said, shaking her head.

"Lisa must be under a lot of stress right now. I bet a break would do her a world of good. Let's write and see if she can come to the Halloween party," Palmer suggested.

A bright grin lit Shanon's face, and her big hazel eyes sparkled happily. "That makes two superior ideas from you in one night," she said, linking arms with Palmer. "Let's do it right now."

"Aren't you coming, Amy?" Palmer asked as they headed for one of the small bedrooms.

"In a minute," Amy murmured, her attention caught by the forlorn expression on Maxie's face. In their concern for their former suitemate, Amy realized that the original Foxes had unwittingly shut out the current one. And she had a sudden uncomfortable feeling that this wasn't the first time they'd done it.

Retrieving her guitar, Amy plopped down on the pink loveseat to practice while she tried to figure out how to handle the sticky situation.

"You're pretty good," Maxie said, looking up from her work. "Isn't that song from *Les Misérables*?"

Amy nodded. "Professor Bernard, my singing teacher, assigns a lot of work from Broadway shows. I really like this one, but it's so sad it always makes me cry."

"You'd better quit before you rust your guitar strings," Maxie advised, deadpan.

Amy smiled at the small joke. Putting her instrument

aside, she walked over to the desk. "You must be getting a jump on the social studies paper that's due next month."

"I probably should be, but I'm not nearly that organized," Max admitted. "I'm working on a comedy skit for the kids."

Amy's dark brows peaked with curiosity. "What kids?"

"The ones who moved into the Alma Meeting House after the big fire in Brighton last month," Maxie explained. "The faculty set up a day-care center for the preschoolers whose mothers work," she explained, "and I volunteered to help out there."

Amy was vaguely aware that the Meeting House now sheltered ten homeless families, but she'd had no idea the program was that extensive. "You spend your free time baby-sitting?" she asked, giving Max an admiring look.

"More like clowning around. I really enjoy it, though. For some reason, little kids seem to like me."

Amy couldn't miss the wistfulness in Maxie's voice. She made a mental note to be more appreciative of her suite-mate in the future. "Are you planning to go into show business when you grow up?"

"One comedian in the family is three too many," Max responded with a grin. "Besides, most audiences are too tough for me. I'm only at my best with short people who're missing their front teeth." Her face softened as she added eagerly, "The kids love music. Maybe you and I could work up an act together: the musical comedy team of Schloss and Ho. Wait—make that Ho and Schloss. We're so desperate for volunteers at the center I'd even be willing to give you top billing."

"It sounds great, but the extra singing lessons I'm taking from Professor Bernard are really pressing me," Amy explained regretfully. "I could ask around the music department, though. Some of the students might have spare time to volunteer."

The light faded from Maxie's face before Amy even finished her reply. "That would be fine," Max said politely. Feigning an exaggerated yawn, she rose from her seat to stretch. "I think I'd better go to bed now. All of a sudden, I'm beat."

As Max walked away, head down and feet dragging, Amy felt a fierce pang of guilt. She was on the verge of following to apologize, but instinct told her that the last thing Max wanted was sympathy. Unfortunately, at the moment, sympathy was all Amy had to offer. Her own schedule was so overwhelming it was all she could do to keep it together.

Heaving a sigh of frustration, she slumped down at the desk and rolled a fresh sheet of paper into the typewriter.

*Dear John,*

*Have you ever had one of those days where no matter what you do, it's wrong? When you walk through a field of wildflowers and discover halfway across that a herd of cows just left a few minutes before you got there?*

*My life seems to be filled with good intentions that go haywire. The due date on my library books is always a week ago. I tie strings around my finger, but then I forget what they're meant to remind me of.*

*How in the world did I let myself get so bogged down? It really hurts when someone reaches out to me and I can't find a spare five minutes to help them. . . .*

Amy stopped typing as an eerie sensation suddenly came

over her, raising the hairs at the nape of her neck. She glanced uneasily around the empty sitting room, but everything checked out normal. With a nervous shrug she turned back to the words she had just typed. The letter seemed a bit too "down," and she decided to go for a more positive ending.

*Whenever I'm in a slump, though, I think of my Uncle Chan, who broke his front tooth while eating oysters. If you haven't already guessed, the up side of the story is that he had chomped down on a pearl!*

*Write soon and let me know how your life's going.*

*All my best,*
*Amy*

As she was searching for a stamp, Amy's attention was captured by a scrabbling noise. When it was joined by a muffled thud against the sitting-room door, she straightened up, nerves on full alert.

"Is someone there?" she called.

There was no answer, so she got up and started across the room to investigate. A yard from the door, another bump stopped her in her tracks.

"Who's out there?" she demanded in a louder tone.

"What are you yelling about?" Palmer yelled, running in from their bedroom.

"I'm not sure," Amy squeaked, her gaze glued to the floor in front of the entrance. As she watched, a white envelope inched its way into the suite.

"What on earth happened? You're as pale as a ghost," Shanon observed as she and Maxie hurried into the sitting room.

15

"Never say ghost to a person who's just been scared out of her wits," Amy giggled, pointing to the envelope. "Somebody—or something—just slid that under the door."

"Doo-doo-doo-doo, doo-doo-doo-doo," Maxie offered her rendition of the theme from the *Twilight Zone*.

"You two have been watching too many horror movies," Palmer said, marching over to snatch open the door. After surveying both ends of the empty hall, she picked up the envelope. "It's for you, Max," she reported, shutting the door.

"You've got to be kidding." Maxie ripped open the envelope with impatient fingers. As she scanned the letter, her initial puzzlement changed to amusement.

"What does it say?" and "Who is it from?" Amy and Shanon asked at the same time.

"C'mon, Max. Don't keep us in suspense," Palmer urged.

Maxie waved them to silence and then read the hand-printed note aloud.

*Dear Max,*
> *Roses are red, your eyes are green.*
> *You're the funniest girl I have ever seen.*
> > *Can I be your pen pal?*

"That sounds like a poem *you* might've written, Max. You didn't have the letter delivered to yourself, did you?" Shanon asked.

"No way! Honest! I don't know who sent this—or how he got it here."

16

"He?" Amy immediately pounced on the pronoun. "How do you know it came from a boy?"

"Because it's obviously a response to the ad we ran in the Ardsley *Lion*," Maxie said, passing the letter to her suitemates for inspection. "Check out the P.S."

As the note moved from hand to hand, each girl's mouth dropped open in amazement.

Just as Max's ad had ended with "P.S. I'm a girl," the mysterious pen pal had written, "P.S. I'm a boy."

# CHAPTER 3

There was a moment of stunned silence in Suite 3-D: the possibility that an Ardsley boy had actually been the mystery postman was too exciting for words. Palmer was the first to regain her voice. "The fact that the writer copied Max's P.S. doesn't prove a thing. A lot of Alma girls subscribe to the Ardsley paper, and I say one of them is playing a joke," she deduced.

"For sure. No Ardsley guy in his right mind would risk sneaking into this dorm at night," Shanon agreed. "If he got caught, he could be expelled from school."

"Only if he was lucky," Amy piped up. "Our dearly beloved headmistress might think expulsion was too mild a punishment to fit the crime! You know how strict Miss Pryn can be when it comes to boys."

Maxie shrugged. "I didn't say he actually delivered the letter himself. Maybe he asked a friend or relative who lives here to slip it under the door."

"In which case, you definitely don't want to get involved with him. Who wants a pen pal who's too cheap to buy stamps?" Palmer snorted.

"Maybe he just did it this way to get my attention," Maxie suggested.

"This is as terrific as it is weird," Shanon enthused. "There's only one thing I don't understand. You've never been to Ardsley, so how would this person know that your eyes are green and that you're funny?"

"That's easy. Whoever delivered the note described me to him and passed on a few of the jokes I tell in the dining hall," Maxie concluded. "I bet he—"

"Is this a private conversation, or can anyone join in?"

The startled Foxes all turned around at the sound of the teasing voice. Twelve-year-old Georgette Durand stood in the doorway, her pretty face alive with curiosity.

Palmer frowned at the intruder. With all the good boarding schools in America, she still didn't see why her younger stepsister had insisted on coming to Alma. "It's polite to knock before you come in," she said before any of her suitemates could respond.

"I did, but you were all so busy talking I guess you didn't hear me," Georgette replied, bouncing uninvited into the suite. "Here," she said, handing Palmer a flat, white box. "Mom sent you a present," she explained.

"How nice," Palmer said dully.

"It's a hand-painted silk scarf," Georgette revealed, turning to Amy. "My mother is an artist, you know, and she's learning Chinese brush painting from a man who was born in Taiwan."

"I've got an uncle who is an artist there. I wonder if her teacher knows him," Amy responded with enthusiasm. Then, surreptitiously jabbing an elbow into her roommate's ribs, she said, "Open the box, Palmer. We're all dying to see your gift."

19

As Palmer reluctantly lifted the lid, her sour expression was replaced by one of admiration. The pale lavender silk rectangle was adorned with a delicate flight of blue butterflies. "It's gorgeous," she breathed, immediately draping the lovely scarf around her shoulders. "As you all can see, my stepmother, Alicia, is a very talented person."

"It'll be fabulous with your new blue shirt. And the butterflies' wings are the same color as your eyes," Maxie observed, touching the delicate material with careful fingers.

"Mom painted a bouquet of irises on my scarf—they're my favorite flowers," Georgette confided.

Palmer's smile reflected genuine pleasure. "I really love it. I'll call Alicia tomorrow to thank her."

"She won't be home. I talked to Dad this afternoon, and he said they're going to San Diego for the weekend. He was going to phone you, too, but I told him not to bother—I'd give you the message."

Palmer shot Georgette a sharp look. She was furious. Her stepsister was trying to put as much distance as possible between Palmer and her father. And what about her dad? Why didn't he want to talk to her?

"How very thoughtful of you," Palmer said dryly. All her delight in the gift had vanished. Stripping it from her shoulders, she folded the scarf with exaggerated care and returned it to the box.

The awkward silence that followed the exchange didn't seem to affect Georgette. "What were you guys talking about when I came in?" she asked guilelessly.

"An answer to the ad I ran in the *Lion*," Maxie supplied. As she related the details of the mysterious special delivery, Georgette's blue eyes widened with excitement.

"This is *sooo* romantic," the younger girl sighed, clasping her hands together in utter bliss. "He must really want to be your pen pal if he went to all that trouble."

"Don't be silly," Palmer said irritably. "It's perfectly obvious that someone in this dorm is playing a practical joke on Max."

"I don't think so," Amy disagreed. "This looks like a boy's handwriting to me."

"It doesn't matter anyway. Max got fifteen responses to her ad through the real mail, Georgette," Shanon revealed. "She doesn't need to answer a letter that was shoved under the door."

"That's what you think," Maxie said. "Anyone who's creative enough to think up this bit deserves some consideration. In fact, I'm going to write back this very minute. Otherwise, we'll never know whether it's for real or just a joke. You all can help, if you want to."

"Does that invitation include me?" Georgette asked eagerly.

"You bet. Lights out is forty-five minutes from now, so we'd better get started," Maxie instructed.

Palmer wasn't thrilled to have her stepsister in on the fun, but there was no way to get rid of her without causing a fuss. Muttering under her breath, she joined the group clustered around the desk.

*Dear Pen Pal—*

"Don't call him that," Shanon advised. "You shouldn't commit yourself before you know who this person is."

Maxie dutifully scratched out the salutation and began again.

*Dear Mystery Postman,*

> *You pegged me right—I am a big clown,*
> *And you're sure the slickest guy around.*
> *But before this friendship can go very far,*
> *I've got to know who in the world you are.*
>                              *Yours curiously,*
>                              *Maxie Schloss*

"That's perfect," Amy congratulated her. "But I just thought of one very large problem. How are you going to get it to him?"

"Beats me." Maxie stared at her for a moment, then came up with, "I suppose I could send it through the ghost office."

Shanon giggled. "How about by phony express?"

"Hold it! This is very serious," Georgette cut through the merriment. "If he left your letter by the door without further instructions or a forwarding address," she continued primly, "the most logical thing to do would be to leave your reply in the same spot."

Palmer rolled her gaze to the ceiling. "Thank you, Miss Know-It-All," she muttered under her breath.

"That's a brilliant idea, Georgette," Maxie said.

"Thank you," the younger girl said modestly. A speculative gleam erased the innocence from her eyes as she added, "If you pick this boy, what are you going to do with the other fifteen letters you received from Ardsley?"

"Nothing, I guess," Maxie said. "Why?"

"It seems a pity to let them go to waste. It must be great fun to have an Ardsley correspondent, and I—"

"Actually, all the other letters were from nerds. You wouldn't be the least bit interested," Palmer interrupted her stepsister. She wasn't about to let Georgette become a permanent part of the Foxes' mail call routine. Hustling her out into the hall, she added, "I'm sure you've got a million things to do before lights out, so we won't keep you. Thanks for dropping by with the scarf. I'll be sure to write your mom a thank-you note."

"She could have had the letters if she wanted them," Maxie said as Palmer closed the door firmly behind her stepsister.

"If she wants a pen pal, let her run her own ad," Palmer snapped. Then, without another word, she marched off into her bedroom.

"What's wrong with Palmer?" Maxie asked. "She really seems upset."

Amy darted a sympathetic look toward the closed bedroom door. "She really looks forward to talking with her father. If you ask me, Georgette was way out of line telling Mr. Durand not to bother with the second call."

"Do you think Georgette actually meant to hurt Palmer?" Maxie asked.

Shanon lifted her shoulders in a helpless shrug. "Whether she meant to or not, she definitely did. Maybe we should go talk to Palmer."

Amy shook her head. "I don't think so. It might be better to let her work it out in her own way."

And in the bedroom, that's exactly what Palmer was doing.

*Dear Sam,*
*Sometimes my stepsister drives me bonkers. One minute she's all sweetness and light, and the next she sneaks up and zaps me.*

23

I don't really hate her—I just can't quite figure her out. Part of me really wants a sister to share things with—I just wish it could be someone else! I guess a shrink would call that sibling rivalry, but then, what do shrinks know?

Thanks for listening. I don't expect you to come up with any brilliant solutions for the problem—I just needed to blow off a little steam.

Yours always,
Palmer

# CHAPTER 4

—————◆—————

"What am I doing here?" Shanon muttered through gritted teeth, inwardly cursing the impulse that had made her sign up for swimming at the beginning of the term. Although she'd always been afraid of the water, Shanon had finally decided to take the plunge. It hadn't been too bad—at first. She'd actually enjoyed the exercises Coach Barker conducted at the perimeter of Alma's Olympic-sized pool. But that was before the woman marched her students to the high board and ordered them to jump into the deep end!

Shanon headed toward the edge of the diving board at a snail's pace, staring fearfully at the glassy blue surface below. The water seemed a thousand miles away. Coach Barker's instructions had been very clear: enter the water feetfirst, drop down to kick against the bottom of the pool, then pop up to the top. Piece of cake, right?

Wrong! All at once, the muscles in Shanon's calves locked and her knees turned to jelly.

"Don't think about it, Davis; just do it," the teacher's command echoed through the cavernous chamber.

Shanon squeezed her eyelids shut and launched her body

into the pool. But somewhere between the end of the board and the water, Coach Barker's instructions flew from her brain. Her belly-flop landing not only squished the air from her chest, it neutralized the dive's momentum. Unable to go up or down, Shanon hung in limbo a yard below the surface.

Pure panic expanded her lungs to the maximum, and she sucked in a huge gulp of water. I AM GOING TO DIE! The words were printed in huge, black capitals against the red haze of Shanon's terror. But it wasn't a fast-forward video of her life that flashed across the screen next. It was the clearly focused image of Lisa McGreevy's face.

COACH BARKER ISN'T GOING TO LET YOU DROWN, DUMMY!!

Shanon couldn't tell whether the words came from her own mind or her former roommate's, but the scolding had a calming effect. She kicked against the weight of the water with all the strength she had in her legs. The movement raised her up, but not nearly enough. The air that remained in her chest stung her lungs, then whooshed out in feeble bubbles through her nose.

It seemed as though a thousand years passed before she felt a hand grasp her shoulder.

"Relax and float, Davis," Coach Barker ordered as she pulled Shanon's head above the surface.

"Glub," Shanon spluttered, forcing the muscles in her body to go limp. Miraculously, it worked. She lay spread-eagled atop the water, bobbing along like a cork.

"Way to go, Shanon," her suitemates encouraged as she caught the rung of the ladder and hauled herself out of the pool.

\*　　\*　　\*

"You really had us worried for a while," Amy said as the four Foxes walked back toward the dorm a half hour later.

"Yeah—what were you doing underwater so long?" Palmer asked.

Shanon drew in a deep breath of autumn air, still feeling shaky. "I was just hanging out with a friend."

Maxie shot her a puzzled look. "What's that supposed to mean?"

"You had to be there," Shanon answered, grinning. "Let's get a move on. I'm dying to see if the mystery postman picked up the letter you left by the door this morning."

"Me, too." Palmer took off at a fast trot, calling back over her shoulder, "Last one to the dorm is a dirty sock!"

Intent on the race, the group didn't notice Mr. Griffith, their favorite teacher, mounting the front steps of Fox Hall. The romance between the handsome English teacher and Miss Grayson, the girls' French instructor and faculty adviser for Fox Hall, had been one of the top ten items on the Alma grapevine the term before. The couple, now married, was just settling into a cozy apartment in the basement of the dorm.

"Oops!" Amy skidded to a stop, but not in time to avoid sideswiping Mr. Griffith.

The cardboard box he was carrying tumbled to the ground, spilling a shower of manila folders down the stairs.

"I'm so sorry," Amy apologized, quickly dropping to her knees to recover the papers.

"That's okay. But next time you want to pass in traffic, toot your horn," he teased good-naturedly. "While you're salvaging my life's work, I'll run back to the office and pick up another load. I'm still hoping to get all my

27

files moved into the new apartment before this term is over!"

As he hurried off, Shanon, Palmer, and Maxie pitched in to help Amy. The four were almost finished with the task when Gracie, the terrier puppy that had been the dorm's wedding gift to the newlyweds, arrived on the scene. Gracie jumped from one girl to the other, licking their faces, barking in mock ferocity, and generally making a nuisance of herself.

"Cut it out," Shanon scolded when Gracie clamped onto the hem of her skirt.

As she struggled to pull free, a small pair of hands gently disengaged the dog's teeth, then shooed the squirming puppy away. Shanon straightened up to thank her rescuer.

The boy standing beside her looked to be eight or nine, but his large, dark eyes seemed very old. A thick thatch of black curls framed his small face, and the arms that extended from his too-short jacket sleeves were painfully thin.

"Hi, there. What's your name?" Shanon asked.

He stared at her wordlessly, his expression taut and sullen.

Maxie walked up behind the youngster and playfully tousled his hair. "How's it going, tiger?"

Though he didn't answer, the tension in the boy's jaw relaxed a bit. Without warning, he scooped up an armload of the files they had replaced in the box and darted away.

"Come back here! Those don't belong to you," Palmer called after him.

"It's all right. He tags after Mr. Griffith all the time. He must be helping with the move," Maxie said, watching the child disappear into Fox Hall.

Amy's expression held curiosity mixed with pity. "Poor little guy looks like he could use a few square meals. I wonder who he is?"

"One of the kids who lives in the Meeting House," Maxie supplied. "His name is Jose Hurt, and he acts pretty weird most of the time. While I'm reading to his brothers and sisters, he hides someplace strange—like under a table. He never says a word, but I can tell he's always listening."

"Max is doing volunteer work with the homeless children," Amy explained, quickly filling the other girls in on the shelter situation.

Shanon was definitely impressed. "What a neat thing to do! If I weren't so tied up with *The Ledger,* I'd volunteer, too."

"Not me. I'm not very good around kids. And besides, having ten families jammed together in one place must make an awful mess," Palmer said with a delicate shudder. "I don't know how you can stand it."

Maxie bit back the sarcastic retort that rose to her lips. After all, Palmer had been rich all her life, so how could she be expected to understand poverty? "They're the ones who have it rough," she said simply. "They're mostly farm workers, so the houses that were destroyed in the fire didn't belong to them in the first place. They'll be moving on to another area as soon as the fall apple harvest is finished," she explained.

"Oh." The lone syllable ended Palmer's interest in the subject. "Let's get this box inside so we can check the mail," she said, moving on to something more relevant to her.

It took both Amy and Shanon to carry the carton into

the dorm. Parking it beside the door of the Grayson-Griffiths' apartment, they jogged back outside. Then all four suitemates headed over to Booth Hall to check the student mailboxes.

"We all hit the jackpot today," Palmer reported, holding up a fistful of envelopes.

As Maxie read the return address on her letter, an anxious smile flickered across her face. "It's from Paul Grant."

"That's terrific! I knew he'd come through," Shanon crowed, glancing at the envelope Palmer handed her. The familiar handwriting on the front raised a lump in her throat. The letter was from Lisa. At the same time, she felt a twinge of disappointment. Though it had come to her box number, it was addressed to "The Foxes of the Third Dimension."

The girls hurried back to 3-D to read their mail. The first sight that greeted them there was the letter they'd taped to the door early that morning.

"Rats! I was sure it would be gone by now," Max said gloomily.

Palmer gave her an exasperated look. "What do you care if your mysterious writer doesn't show up? Paul Grant will be a much better pen pal than some creep who goes sneaking around the halls in the dead of night."

Palmer reached up to peel off the tape that still held the envelope, but Maxie waved her away. "Let it stay there," she said. "He may show up yet."

"In the meantime, why don't you open your letter from Paul," Shanon said when the girls were comfortably settled in a circle on the sitting-room floor.

Maxie slid a sidewise peek at the door before she ripped open the envelope and read:

*Dear Max,*

*I guess the best word to describe me is* ordinary. *I'm kind of on the tall side, and though I'm no superstar on the basketball court, I do shoot a lot of hoops for fun. As you know, I've got blond hair, green eyes, and a B average. I guess that about sums it up.*

*Except for two things: I'm a pretty fair SCUBA diver and I'm nuts about ancient ruins. I can't decide whether I want to be a marine biologist or an archaeologist when I get out of school. Maybe I'll do both!*

*I'm sure you got dozens of answers to your ad, but if it's not too late, I'd like to be your pen pal.*

> *Hoping to hear from you soon,*
> *Paul Grant*

"He sounds really neat," Amy approved.

Shanon nodded her enthusiastic agreement. "And definitely sincere. Mars says Paul is one of the nicest guys at Ardsley."

"He's certainly got my vote," Palmer chimed in. "What do you say, Max? Is it a done deal?"

Maxie squirmed under the weight of their hopeful gazes. As much as she wanted to please her suitemates, she really wasn't sure about this whole boy-girl business. While she could probably handle writing to a guy like Paul Grant, meeting him face-to-face was a very different story. "He's one of my top two candidates," she hedged, leaning forward to check the door again. "But I'd still like to find out who delivered the letter last night before I make the final decision."

"I guess that's fair," Amy said, suppressing a surge of impatience. "Okay, let's see what John's been up to lately."

31

*Dear Amy,*

*I just received a funny card from the people I got to know when I worked as a messenger in my dad's law office this summer. They used to call me "Bumbles the Cat" because even though I goofed things up, I somehow always managed to land on my feet. One time I delivered an important brief to Judge Brooks instead of Judge Banks. Lucky for me, Banks was home with the flu and Brooks took his cases. And I was sure my goose was cooked when I accidentally set off the building's security alarm system. But when the police came, they nabbed a thief who'd broken into one of the other offices. I was a super-hero that day!*

*I'm sure there's a song in all of this. Why don't you take a crack at the first verse?*

*Your collaborator,*
*John (aka Bumbles)*

"It's really weird how our minds run in the same direction," Amy said, grinning as she folded the note. "Your turn, Palmer."

*Dear Palmer,*

*One of the guys in the band—Zack—has a brother who got into trouble with drugs. For some reason, Zack felt really guilty about it—as if he could have stopped him somehow. Zack was getting himself messed up. But talking to me made him feel better. It made me feel kind of special.*

*The whole thing started me thinking about the future. I've always wanted to be a professional musician, but*

*maybe I have a knack for counseling. Drop me a line to let
me know what you think.*

*Truly and always,*
*Sam*

*P.S. I think Alma Stephens's temporary shelter is making a
fantastic contribution to the community. I've joined a
group in my school that's been collecting food and clothing
for some of the other homeless families. I'm sure you're
also helping as much as you can.*

"Sam, the shrink—works for me. Psychiatrists make
tons of money," Palmer gloated. But her satisfied smile
warmed as she turned to Shanon. "You go now. It's time
for Lisa's letter."

The eager expressions on her suitemates' faces reminded
Maxie that she was still an outsider. Not wanting to in-
trude on what was clearly the main event of the session,
she tactfully edged a few inches away from the circle.

There was a note of wistfulness in Shanon's voice as she
began to read the typewritten note from the missing Fox.

*Hi, gang,*
  *School is mostly okay. I've started taking my lunch from
home so I won't have to eat the junk they serve in the
cafeteria. There's a girl in my class who reminds me of
Muffin Talbot. She's really tiny and always wears pink.
Every time I look at her, I remember Muff's tacky pink
curtains. That's it for now. I'll write again soon.*

*Hugs for everybody,*
*Lisa*

"What a bummer," Palmer said. "She didn't say one word about what's happening between her parents. I wonder if they're still arguing all the time."

Amy heaved a sigh and rose to her feet. "I guess no news is good news. The last time she mentioned them, Lisa said her mom and dad were seeing a marriage counselor. Maybe the therapy is working."

As the others wandered off to get ready for dinner, Shanon sat staring down at a line that had been dashed off in red ink at the bottom of the note.

*P.S. especially for Shanon: Thanks for caring so much. Your letters help keep my head above water.*

*Love,*
*L.*

Shanon's thoughts immediately flashed back to the incident in the swimming pool. It could have been just an eerie coincidence, but she preferred to believe in the strong bond that tied her to Lisa.

"Don't worry, pal. Coach Davis isn't going to let you drown," she murmured softly.

# CHAPTER 5

If the dinner entree of the evening had been entered in a bake-off, Mrs. Worth, Alma's popular cook and dietician, would surely have walked away with the blue ribbon. The flaky crust of her pot pie was as light as an angel's wings, the creamy filling of chicken and vegetables savory and satisfying.

Maxie dug into her strawberry shortcake, blissfully closing her eyes at the first sweet bite. "If I keep this up, I'm going to be the exact size and shape of the Goodyear blimp."

"Hi, group," Georgette interrupted, bouncing over with her dessert. Without waiting for an invitation, she borrowed a chair from a neighboring table and shoved it into the space beside her stepsister. Plopping down, she confided, "I should go back and do some homework before the dorm meeting tonight, but since I'm already two weeks ahead in every subject, I suppose it won't hurt to take a break. You don't mind if I join you, do you?"

"Would it do any good if we did?" Palmer huffed.

"That's a beautiful blouse you're wearing, Georgette,"

Shanon said quickly, giving the girl a welcoming smile.

"Thanks. It's handmade. Dad brought it back from a business trip to Mexico City," Georgette reported, absently fingering the dainty embroidery on the front. "I know it's a bit summery for September, but wearing it makes me feel less homesick."

"If you miss California so much, maybe you should consider going back," Palmer advised helpfully.

"I wouldn't dream of leaving Alma Stephens. Being with my big sister is so much fun," Georgette responded. Smiling serenely, she pushed back her chair and rose from the table. "I really should go to the bio lab and put in a few hours on my experiment. Mom and Dad are so proud of my grades; I wouldn't want to let them down."

Palmer's narrowed gaze followed her stepsister's retreat from the table. *Had that been another zinger?* she wondered darkly. No longer hungry, she pushed her dessert away. "If everyone has finished pigging out," she said, "let's get back to the dorm."

"Fine with me," said Amy. "I can't wait to see if the mystery postman is on the job."

He wasn't. When the girls got back to Suite 3-D, they found Maxie's envelope still taped in place. Disappointed, Max followed the others into the suite.

"Leave the door open, just in case," Amy advised. "Let's all do our homework in the sitting room so we can watch for him."

Maxie's shoulders lifted in a shrug. "It's no big deal," she said. "If he doesn't come tonight, I may just forget about the whole thing and start writing to Paul," she added, trying her best to be casual.

But it was evident that the letter *was* a big deal—and not

36

just to Maxie. For the next twenty minutes, she, Shanon, and Amy spent more time staring at the entrance than at their books.

Still huffy over her stepsister's parting shot, Palmer flounced over to the loveseat and snatched up the latest issue of *Seventeen,* grumbling, "This is a total waste of time." But even she kept one eye on the door as she flipped through the pages of the magazine.

It wasn't long before the vigil was rewarded by a sudden flash of motion outside. All the girls jumped to their feet at once, but Maxie was first to reach the door. "Gotcha!" she yelled, jerking it open.

Palmer's stepsister stood in the hallway, her small face solemn. "Can I come in for a minute?"

"Sure thing," Maxie said, trying to hide her disappointment. As she ushered the younger girl into the suite, she made sure not to close the door completely.

"I came to apologize for the crack I made in the dining hall," Georgette told Palmer. "I didn't mean to give you the impression that Dad's not proud of you, too. He's always telling people how beautiful you are and how much he loves you."

Palmer's jaw dropped. Though the words sounded sincere, she found it almost impossible to trust her stepsister. "Forget about it," she said grudgingly. "It's no big deal."

"I'd really like for us to be friends," her stepsister continued when Palmer turned back to her magazine.

"I've never exactly thought of you as my enemy," Palmer said noncommittally.

Georgette breathed a sigh of relief. "Now that that's settled, I'd like to know if you'll all be at the dorm meeting tomorrow night. I'm definitely going, but I'm not quite sure what to expect. Can you fill me in on what it will be like?"

"No problem," Shanon said quickly. "Maggie—I mean Ms. Grayson-Griffith—just goes over the dorm rules to make sure everyone understands them; then she talks about the various student committees—"

"Speaking of which, your sister is going to volunteer to be Fox Hall's social chairperson this year," Maxie announced. "She's got the greatest idea for a—"

"—fund-raising activity. We're all going to collect junk and take it to Brighton's recycling plant," Palmer broke in before Max could reveal her real plan. And with that, she hustled Georgette out into the hall. "Be sure to tell everyone you know to save their empty soda cans," she called after her.

Palmer shut the door firmly, leaning against it with a low whistle of relief. "That was a close one. If Georgette finds out about the Halloween party, she might figure out a way to mess it up."

Amy and Shanon gaped at each other wordlessly. But Maxie couldn't stop herself from blurting, "Give the kid a break, why don't you? It wasn't very nice of you to pretend to accept her apology when you're obviously still mad at her."

Palmer stiffened. "What happens between me and my stepsister is none of your business," she said frostily, turning toward her bedroom.

"Yes it is," Maxie insisted. "I like both of you very much, and I hate to see you trying to sabotage your relationship."

"Max is right. Georgette called a truce, and I think you should at least meet her halfway," Shanon spoke up.

"It's obvious that she considers you her role model," Amy added her two cents' worth. "And deep down inside, you don't really dislike her, do you?"

Some of the anger drained from Palmer's face. "No, I don't. But we're just too different to get along. Besides being totally boy and clothes crazy, Georgette *always* has to have her own way. And she's also way too spoiled, selfish, insensitive, and short."

Amy and Shanon exchanged a secret glance of amusement. Except for the height part, their suitemate had described herself to a tee.

Maxie looked at Palmer unblinkingly. "All that may be true, but I think she really cares about you. Won't you please give her a chance to prove it?"

Palmer met Maxie's bright green gaze. She considered the request for a moment, then nodded "yes." "I suppose it won't hurt to give it a shot. I'll tell her I—"

"What was that?" Amy suddenly broke into the conversation. "Did you guys hear a noise out in the hall?"

"The mailman!" Maxie gasped.

The four Foxes stumped all over each other in their haste to get to the entrance. But they were too late: the hallway was empty—and the letter was gone.


"I think this mystery postman business is one of the most exciting things that has ever happened in Fox Hall," Shanon said the next morning as she and her suitemates trooped down the front steps of the dorm.

"You've got that right," Amy agreed, peering hopefully back over her shoulder as if to spot the secret pen pal. "Imagine having a guy risking his neck to deliver a letter!"

"It's not a guy, it's a girl," Palmer insisted for the umpteenth time. "And if we don't get a move on, we're going to miss breakfast."

The girls picked up their pace and were halfway across the quadrangle when a shout from behind stopped them in their tracks.

Mr. Griffith trotted up to join them. Still jogging in place, he pulled a crumpled envelope from his sweat-suit pocket and handed it to Maxie. "When I left the dorm this morning, I found that by the flowerpot on the front stoop," he panted before taking off again.

"Thanks—I think," Maxie called after him.

"Is it from . . . ?" Shanon's voice trailed off, too excited to finish the question.

Maxie peered at her name scrawled on the front. "Looks like the same handwriting."

"Well, don't just stand there. Open it up!" Palmer commanded.

Maxie swallowed hard and obeyed.

*Dear Max,*

*My first is in a practickle joke, but never in a riddle. My second is in an onion and a potato. My third lives in Mississippi but never goes to Ohio, and my fourth is the beginning of everything. Put that all together and you'll know who I am.*

*Your pen pal.*
*P.S. If nickels are made of nickel, shouldn't we call pennies coppers?*

Shanon's forehead wrinkled with puzzlement. "What's that all about?"

40

"Beats me," Amy said. "I wish we knew who this guy is."

"We will when we figure out the riddle," Maxie said, her eyes bright with excitement.

"Do we really want to?" Palmer asked dubiously. "His spelling is almost as bad as his penmanship. My handwriting was better than that when I was in the fourth grade."

"He's got a good sense of humor and his riddle sounds really clever. That's more important to me than how he spells," Maxie countered. Turning back toward Fox Hall, she said, "You all go on to the dining hall. I want to work on the riddle a while before my first class."

As Max walked slowly back across the quad, rereading the crumpled note, the other three girls passed around a knowing glance.

"She's really getting caught up in this," Shanon said. "I hope her secret pen pal is as terrific in person as he is on paper."

Palmer was less enthusiastic. "It would be better for us if she dumped the mailman and concentrated on Paul Grant."

Amy shook her head. "It would be nice, but there's no point in pushing her. No matter what we say, Max is going to do exactly as she pleases."

"I just hope she knows what she's doing," Palmer said doubtfully.

# CHAPTER 6

Dear Sam,

Psychiatry would be a fabulous career for you! I'm sure you'd have zillions of patients—all paying top dollar for your services, of course.

You'll be glad to know I'm going to patch things up with Georgette. She really looks up to me as her older sister, so I've decided to give her a break.

I agree that the shelter thing is very nice. If my schedule weren't so tight, I'd love to help those poor people. Our suitemate, Max Schloss—you met her at the book fair last month—works with the children who live in the Meeting House. Max is a good person, even though she gets a little bossy sometimes. As you already know, she's also drop-dead gorgeous, but I try not to hold that against her. Ha-ha!

At the moment, the big mission in my life is to make our dormitory a truly fun place. I'm volunteering to be chair-person of the social committee. Keep October 31st free—this is your unofficial invitation to the first annual Fox Hall Halloween party!

*Got to run now. I'm busy, busy, busy these days.*

*Socially yours,*
*Palmer*

Ten minutes before closing time, Amy struggled up to the librarian's desk to deposit an armload of long-overdue books. "I'm afraid these are a teeny bit late, Ms. Jones. Can you tell me how much my fine will be?" she asked, fumbling through her backpack for her wallet.

The librarian flipped to the cards in the pockets of each volume, tsk-tsking as she jotted an ominously long column of figures on a scrap of paper. Amy dropped her gaze to the toes of her running shoes as she did some mental arithmetic of her own. Including the three pennies she had found trapped in the lining of her jacket, her total assets were $2.47.

"That comes to five dollars and ninety-four cents," Ms. Jones finally announced disapprovingly. "However, you won't have to pay a fine this time. We're having an amnesty all week."

Amy felt a huge grin spread over her face. *John's not the only cat who has nine lives,* she thought. *His luck must be rubbing off on me!* At that moment, the first verse of the new song magically popped into her head. She pressed her hand over her mouth, but too late to catch the giggle.

The librarian pinned her with a stern look. "Keeping books out past the due date is no laughing matter," she said. "I do hope you won't let this happen again."

"Yes, ma'am—I mean—no, ma'am," Amy stammered, beating a hasty retreat. She was almost at the door when she spotted Shanon seated in the reading room. Veering off course, she hurried over, swiped a sheet of paper, and, plucking the pen from her suitemate's fingers, began to write:

*Dear John,*
   *How's this for a start? It's a rap song.*
      *Gather round me, gang, and listen to this beat*
      *let me introduce you to a guy who's really neat*
               *captain fixit—captain fixit*
      *the only super-hero who has two left feet!*

   *The ball is in your court now, Bumbles the Cat. What-ever you do, don't drop it!*
                                    *Write back A.S.A.P.*
                                    *Amy*

Shanon's unsuccessfully smothered chuckles brought a chorus of *Sh-h-h-h*'s from a nearby table. "Terrific! I can't wait to see what John comes up with," she whispered. And pushing her notebook in front of Amy, she added, "See what you think of this."

*Dear Mars,*
   *The letters I'm getting from Lisa are shorter and shorter. Pretty soon now, "Dear Shanon" and "Love, Lisa" will be on the same line. I've heard that she isn't communicating very much with Reggie, either. Is she still writing to Rob? I'm sure that sharing her problems with her friends would do Lisa a world of good, but I can't get her to open up to me. Maybe if we all got together, we could brainstorm a plan.*
   *On the up side, I'm finding a whole lot to like about Maxie. Underneath the comedy act she puts on, she's a real*

*person and fun. She spends most of her free time enter-*
*taining the kids at Alma's homeless shelter. She's good*
*for the Foxes, too. Palmer has a tendency to steamroller*
*people, but Maxie has started challenging her just the*
*way Lisa used to do. It's good to have some balance*
*back in 3-D.*

*That's all I have time for now. Please let me know what's*
*going with you—and if you have any suggestions for help-*
*ing Lisa, please send them along.*

*Your friend,*
*Shanon*

"You must've been reading my mind. Maxie deserves a
definite round of applause for getting Palmer to agree to a
truce with Georgette," Amy said, smiling as she finished
the note. "How long do you think it will last?"

"A week or so, if we're lucky," Shanon predicted, crossing her fingers. "I almost forgot. Palmer and Maxie are
picking us up here so we won't have to go back to 3-D
before the dorm meeting."

No sooner were the words out of her mouth than the
other two Foxes hurried into the reading room and over to
the table.

"Have you solved the riddle yet, Max?" Amy asked.

"No, but I've got a good start. The—"

"Hold it down, will you? I'm trying to study," a dark-
haired girl at the next table looked up from her book to
warn.

"Let's go back in the stacks where we can talk without
disturbing anyone," Palmer whispered, motioning the others to follow her.

When they were all crowded around a table in the back

of the library, Maxie continued her explanation. "There are four letters in his name." She spread out the letter Mr. Griffith had found. "Listen to this," she said. " 'My second is in an onion and a potato.' The only letter those words have in common is O."

Light dawned in Amy's eyes. "His fourth is 'the beginning of everything'—that must be an E," she deduced excitedly.

"You got it," Maxie said. "The first and third still have me stumped, but I answered his note anyway. Listen to this."

*Dear Mystery Mailman,*

*You have a great future with the C.I.A.! Even though I haven't finished cracking your code, trying has been great fun.*

*I'm very glad to have you for a pen pal because you make me laugh and think, both at the same time.*

*By the way, haven't you heard the old gag about the bank robber who called a penny a copper? The crook got arrested!*

*Okay, so it's a terrible joke. What do you expect for a few cents?*

*Looking forward to your next letter,*
*Max*
*P.S. Maybe you'd better not sneak into Fox Hall again. If you got caught, we'd both be in big trouble.*

"Good move," Shanon approved the postscript.

Amy nodded. "Yeah, but now we won't be able to watch for him."

"He's obviously crazy about Max. Sooner or later, he's going to want to talk to her in person," Palmer predicted. And glancing at her watch, she added, "We'd better save the rest of the decoding for another time or else we'll be late for the dorm meeting."

The Foxes nearly set a campus record for the cross-quad dash. Maxie made a quick detour past the flowerpot to mail her pen pal letter, then followed the other three into the Fox Hall common room.

Palmer took the lead, elbowing a path through the crowd. The group found seating space on the floor just as Maggie Grayson-Griffith called the meeting to order.

"I know you were looking forward to my lecture on Fox Hall's rules and regulations," she quipped, "but I'm going to save that for our next meeting."

The announcement was greeted with a chorus of cheers. Waving the crowd to silence, the popular young teacher continued: "The first item on our agenda is the Alma Stephens shelter. Our student volunteers are doing a tremendous job, but there's just so much they can do without any financial backing. In addition, I'd like to see Fox Hall sponsor some type of fund-raising activity. Do any of you have any money-making suggestions you'd like to share?"

A hand in the third row immediately waved for attention.

"Tina Penderhew," Maggie said, smiling encouragement.

Georgette's roommate rose to her feet and glanced quickly around the room. "We could collect old newspapers and empty aluminum cans and sell them to the recycling plant in Brighton," she said nervously.

47

"That's a terrific plan. We'd be earning money for a good cause and helping to clean up the environment at the same time," Mrs. Grayson-Griffith approved.

A spontaneous round of applause broke out as Tina sat down again.

Palmer's jaw dropped open with shock. "That was *my* idea!" she leaned over to whisper to Amy. "I'll bet anything my stepsister put her up to it."

"You know you never really intended to start a recycling program, Palmer. You just made it up to keep Georgette from finding out about the Halloween party," Amy reminded her in a low tone.

Palmer's mouth turned down in a pout. "So what? I thought of it first, so I should get the credit."

"Give it a rest, Palmer," Maxie murmured. "When you spring your proposal for the Halloween party, you'll be the absolute star of Fox Hall."

The gavel interrupted the girls' exchange, and Mrs. Grayson-Griffith spoke into the silence. "As you probably have heard, Brenda Smith is resigning as chairperson of the social committee," she announced. "Before we discuss a replacement, I'd like Brenda to stand up so we can give her a big hand for the fine work she did last year," Maggie requested.

The applause was accompanied by appreciative whistles from the crowd. "Thanks, everyone. Sorry I have to flake out on you this year, but my schedule is really squeezing me," Brenda explained, smiling as she resumed her seat.

"Heading the social committee is a difficult job. Anyone who takes it on can expect a lot of hard work," Mrs. Grayson-Griffith continued. "Are there any volun—"

Before the words were out of Maggie's mouth, Palmer

48

rose to her feet and walked regally toward the front of the room. As she felt her friends' eyes on her, she lifted her chin proudly. Unfortunately, she lifted it so high that she failed to notice that she wasn't alone. She and Georgette reached the front of the room in a dead heat. The initial buzz from the assembly faded to dead silence as the two Durands faced each other.

Palmer felt her neck go from hot to cold and back again. Although she was so furious she could hardly see straight, she somehow managed to keep a pleasant smile on her face.

"This is family cooperation at its best," Ms. Grayson-Griffith said, stepping between them. And slipping an arm around each girl's shoulders, she continued: "Fox Hall residents, meet your new social committee co-chairpersons. With these two in charge, I'm sure we'll have loads of fun this year."

While the other girls applauded, Georgette gazed innocently at her sister. "I know this is a surprise," she murmured, "but I couldn't let you take on such a heavy load all by yourself. We Durands have to stick together," she said, eagerly extending her hand.

Palmer had no choice but to take it. Squeezing her stepsister's fingers in a viselike grip, she promised herself that no matter what, Georgette was not going to upset her plans for the Halloween party. "We'll do okay just as long as you remember who's really in charge," she muttered under her breath.

# CHAPTER 7

"... So the Prince asked for the Princess's hand in marriage, and they lived happily ever after," Maxie concluded the fairy tale she was reading.

The three children seated around her were quietly absorbing the story until little Becky Hurt blurted out, "Why did the Prince just want to marry her hand? Didn't he like the rest of her?"

The question caught Maxie off guard. Chuckling, she came back with, "Not particularly; but they worked out a package deal before the wedding."

"The stories always end that way," Becky's older sister, Lila, observed thoughtfully. She nibbled at her thumbnail—no easy task with two front teeth missing—and asked, "What do people do when they live happily ever after?"

"In this case, they bought a castle in the suburbs and traded the Prince's horse in for a purple sports car," Maxie improvised an updated ending.

"Yuk! I hate all that mushy love stuff," five-year-old

Billy Hurt complained. "The Prince shoulda chopped the wicked witch to pieces with an axe."

"Next time, I'll read *How the Grinch Stole Christmas*. There's a lot more action in that plot," Maxie promised, playfully tousling his hair. "Or"—she craned her neck to peer at a dark-haired child under the table—"maybe you'd like to pick tomorrow's story, Jose. What would you like to hear?"

The nine-year-old boy returned her inviting gaze with a solemn stare. Without responding, he retreated farther into his favorite hiding place.

Max felt a familiar stirring of frustration. No matter what tactic she tried, she hadn't been able to reach the strange, silent child. "That's all for today, kids," she said quietly, too discouraged to go into her usual Bugs Bunny closing bit. Rising from the circle, she directed the daily clean-up operation: "Billy, you and Becky pick up the crayons while Lila puts away the coloring books."

"It's not fair for us to do all the work. Jose listened to the story, too," Becky said disapprovingly.

"That's a very good point." Tightening her resolve, Maxie dropped to her hands and knees. She peered under the table again, snapping a crisp, "You can put the juice cups in the trash and straighten the chairs, Jose. Nobody gets a free ride around here."

But firmness didn't work any better than diplomacy. Without a word, Jose scrambled out from under the table, then pelted off to hide behind the door.

"I give up," Maxie said to no one in particular as she began collecting the library books she had brought to the session. When she retrieved the thick volume of fairy tales by the Brothers Grimm, an envelope protruding from the pages caught her attention.

"What on earth . . . ?" The question trailed off as she spotted the familiar handwriting on the front. It was a letter from her mysterious pen pal!

When she'd arrived at the shelter two hours earlier, she had seen a group of Ardsley volunteers outside playing football with the older boys who lived in the Meeting House. Bashful around guys her own age, Maxie hadn't paid much attention to the game. She now spun around to survey the room, but she and the four children were alone. Her heart pounding, she ripped open the envelope and scanned the note inside.

*Dear Max,*

*Yesterday, I read a story in a newspaper about starving people. Why do reporters say that Etheeopia is in the Third World? Africa and America are both part of Earth. Since we're all on the same planet, we oughtta take care of each other—nobody should die because they're hungry.*

*The story made me feel like a tornadoe, all whirly and dark inside. But then I remembered how pretty your smile is and the clouds went away. I think you are the nicest person in the whole world.*

*I would never do anything to get you in trouble, so I won't come to Fox Hall again. But if it's okay with you, I'll still keep writing.*

Maxie swallowed hard as the last lines on the page jumped out at her. Her secret pen pal had signed his letter, "Your friend, Jose."

"Jose?" she repeated aloud, her head quickly swiveling

toward the door. But there was no way that strange little boy could be her mystery mailman, she told herself. Dismissing the absurd possibility, she turned to Lila and asked, "Did one of the guys who were playing football come in here while I was reading?"

"Nope."

"Well, did you see somebody stick this envelope in my book?"

"Uh-huh." Caught up in a fit of giggles, Lila pointed to the dark-eyed youngster, who was watching from the doorway. "Jose did it."

The breath Maxie had been holding came out in a startled whoosh. She shifted from foot to foot, her thoughts spinning in a confused jumble. Jose Hurt spent quite a bit of time at the Griffiths' apartment; he could easily have slipped up to the third floor of Fox Hall to deliver the letter. But how would he have known she was looking for a pen pal? And how could a nine-year-old child—particularly one who wouldn't even talk—write such a sensitive and touching letter?

Acting on pure impulse, she hurried over to confront him. But before she was halfway across the room, Jose dashed through the open door.

"Come back here, Jose!" Maxie called, taking off after him. By the time she reached the hallway, though, he was nowhere to be seen.

"Is something wrong?" Mr. Griffith asked, coming up behind her with the frisky Gracie nipping at his heels.

"Yes—I mean no, sir. I was just. . . ." Maxie's voice trailed off, and her face turned bright red as she turned to face the handsome English teacher. She'd had a crush on Dan Griffith from the moment she first laid eyes on him.

"Gracie and I were just on our way back to Fox Hall. If you're finished with story hour, we'd be glad to have you walk with us," he invited.

Cheeks burning, Max nodded happily. "I—I'll g-get my books and jacket," she stammered.

As they strolled slowly through the gathering twilight, Mr. Griffith didn't try to push Maxie into a conversation. After a few minutes, she recovered enough of her composure to ask, "What's wrong with Jose, Mr. G? He won't talk, and he acts like he's mad at the world."

"If he isn't, he certainly has a right to be," the teacher answered, kicking absently at a pile of leaves on the path. "Jose was physically abused when he was younger."

Maxie stopped short, her eyes widening with horror. "Mr. and Mrs. Hurt beat him?"

"No way! As a matter of fact, they saved him," he said, stooping to free the leash from Gracie's collar. As the puppy scampered away, he explained, "The Hurts aren't Jose's real parents. A couple of years ago, they found him abandoned and in pretty bad shape, so they took him in. They've done everything they can to make him forget his painful past, but he still bears deep emotional scars. In spite of all the love and care his foster parents have given him, Jose still refuses to communicate. Mrs. Hurt told me he was always in trouble at school last year. He got into fights with the other kids because they called him stupid."

"He isn't stupid," Maxie protested fiercely.

"Far from it," Mr. Griffith agreed. He stood up, shoving his hands in his pockets. As they resumed their walk across campus, he continued, "Jose is incredibly bright. He reads everything he can get his hands on: books, newspapers—cereal boxes, if there's nothing else handy. He even wanted my copies of the Alma *Ledger* and Ardsley *Lion,* so I gave them to him."

Well, that explained one thing, Maxie thought: the little boy had seen her ad in the *Lion.* Jose Hurt! The name seemed tragically appropriate for the mistreated, solitary child. A wave of pity swept over Maxie, so compelling and intense it nearly took her breath away.

"You care a lot about Jose, don't you?" Mr. Griffith asked, gently patting her shoulder.

"Yes," Maxie said. She hastily wiped a tear from her cheek with the sleeve of her jacket. Embarrassed by her lapse, she added gruffly, "I just wish he would talk to me."

"So do I. We've worked out a system, though. He points to what he wants and I give it to him." The comforting pressure of Mr. Griffith's fingers tightened. "Poor little guy needs all the friends he can get. Don't give up on him, Maxie."

"I won't."

A crescendo of joyous yelps from up ahead broke into the somber moment. Beside herself with puppy love, Gracie was running circles around the approaching Ms. Grayson-Griffith. Maggie knelt to scoop up the wiggling terrier, waving to her husband and Maxie.

"We're going to jog around the softball field before dinner. You're welcome to join us, Max," Mr. Griffith invited.

"Thanks, but my brain needs exercise more than the rest of me," Maxie declined regretfully. "I've got a math quiz tomorrow."

Mr. Griffith started away, then turned back, smiling. "You're a good girl, Maxine Edith Schloss. I think Jose Hurt is lucky to have you on his side."

The unexpected compliment went a long way toward lifting Max's drooping spirits. No matter how hard it was or how long it took, she promised herself, she would find a way to communicate with Jose. As she cut across the campus, it occurred to her that she had already made a breakthrough of sorts. Jose *was* communicating with her— through their letters. And while he showed no interest in speaking, he was all ears whenever she read a story to him and the other children. Perhaps she could be the one person to reach Jose.

Max ran all the way back to Suite 3-D. She pushed open the door and breathlessly waved Jose's letter at her startled suitemates. "You'll never guess what happened at the shelter!"

"You got more mystery mail," Amy said, abandoning her guitar in her excitement.

"Bingo! And this time it's signed."

Before Maxie could fill in the details, Palmer plucked the sheet of paper from her fingers. "The mystery mailman's name is Jose!" she squealed.

"Muffin Talbot told me there were a bunch of Ardsley guys at the Meeting House this afternoon," Shanon said, leaning over Palmer's shoulder to peek at the note. "Did Jose just walk up and hand this to you, Max?"

"No, he slipped it into one of my books, and—"

"Did you at least get a look at him?" Amy interrupted.

"Yes, but—"

"Well, don't just stand there with your mouth hanging open. Tell us what he looks like," Palmer demanded. "Is he cute?"

"He's got black hair and big, dark eyes, and—"

"I *knew* he'd be a hunk," Shanon cut her off. Confiscating the note for a closer look, she sighed, "It's clear that he really likes you, Max. And he's so sensitive and caring."

"You can say that again. I can't imagine John getting this upset about world hunger," Amy admitted a bit enviously. "Jose's obviously the intellectual type."

"And very thoughtful and deep, too. I can tell that from his line about the tornado." Palmer turned her bright blue eyes to the ceiling. "He's probably haunted by some dark secret from his past—just like Heathcliff in *Jane Eyre*."

"*Wuthering Heights*," Amy interjected wryly.

"Whatever." Palmer dismissed the correction with an airy wave of her hand.

The picture was so close to the truth that Maxie nearly laughed. "Jose's a very creative boy, but he—"

"You bet he is!" Amy agreed. "Otherwise he would've gotten caught when he sneaked into the dorm."

"How tall is he?"

"Do his parents have money?"

"Do you think he'll come to our Halloween party?"

The questions were coming so thick and fast that it was impossible for Maxie to field them. "Time out, guys," she lifted her voice above the din. "Don't make a big deal out of this. I think Jose would like to be friends with me, and if I—"

"Don't be so modest. You know he's crazy about you!" Palmer threw her arms around Maxie's shoulders. "This is so great!" she cried. "I'm really happy for you. You've got the best pen pal of all—except for Sam, of course!"

Her other suitemates joined in the bear hug, their congratulations pouring over her. For the first time since moving into 3-D, Maxie felt as if she really belonged there. Thanks to Jose's letters, she was no longer just

Lisa McGreevy's replacement; she was truly one of the Foxes.

But what if she told them that there was no tall, dark, and handsome Ardie who was madly in love with her? Everything would change in a minute. Her suitemates would laugh themselves silly when they found out that her mysterious pen pal was actually an emotionally disturbed nine-year-old! And then they would start bugging her to write Paul Grant again.

"What's Jose's last name?" Shanon asked when the hub-bub had died down.

It wouldn't do any harm to let the game go on just a little longer, Max told herself with a secret smile. Crossing her fingers behind her back, she came up with a response that was technically the truth:

"He never told me."

# CHAPTER 8

———◆———

"Why don't we let Gracie do her own thing for a while?" Palmer panted, plopping down in the shade of a large oak.

A relieved Amy sat down beside her. "The Griffiths need to cut down on that dog's vitamins. We've been running circles around the campus for the past half hour, and she's not even breathing hard."

Kneeling to unsnap the leash from the frisky puppy's collar, Shanon glanced along the path the three girls had chosen. The back side of the Meeting House was just visible through the thinning red and gold foliage. "We shouldn't have come this way," she fretted. "If Max sees us, she'll think we're spying on her."

"We're not exactly spying," Palmer defended. Stretching out on a cushion of dry leaves, she gave her friends an impish grin before adding, "Our inquiring minds are dying to know what Max's mystery man looks like. What better way to find out than by checking out the shelter?"

"We *could* write and ask Mars and John if they know any Joses," Shanon proposed. "It's not a very common name."

Palmer scooped up a double handful of leaves and tossed them in Shanon's lap. "Great idea! Maybe he has dark secrets."

"We are kind of snooping," Shanon admitted with a guilty chuckle. "But so what? While we're waiting, let's read the letters that came today."

"Good plan. I've got a singing lesson in twenty minutes, so I'll go first," Amy said, pulling an envelope from the pocket of her jacket.

*Dear Amy,*

*We're really grooving, partner. Here's the second verse:*

*he can fall into a garbage can, but dig this jive—*
*when they pull him out, he smells just like Chanel*
*Number Five.*

> *captain fixit—captain fixit:*
*no matter what he has to do, the dude will survive!*

*If you need more material, here's another close call I had while I was at home. Dad invited an important client for dinner, and Mom made lasagna. That alone was enough of a disaster—she's the world's worst cook! Anyway, she went out and I forgot that I was supposed to watch the stuff. When I finally looked in the oven, it was half an inch thick and as dry as the Sahara. How did Captain Fixit get out of that one? No sweat! I slapped on six layers of mozzarella and nuked the whole thing in the microwave. Dad's client thought it was a new-wave pizza and asked Mom for the recipe!*

*Looking forward to the next exciting episode.*

Captain John

"This will be the most radical song in the history of

rap," Amy predicted, giggling over her pen pal's letter.

"If we're not careful, your next verse will be about how we lost the Griffiths' dog," Palmer warned, jumping up to retrieve Gracie from a tangle of underbrush. She set the puppy down in Shanon's arms, then took out her own letter.

*Dear Palmer,*

*I'm glad you have enough confidence in me to cast me as the next Sigmund Freud, but I had something a little more realistic in mind. I think I'd like to be a high-school guidance counselor. Although there wouldn't be a Porsche in my parking space, I could get by on the satisfaction of knowing I'd helped some kid stay out of trouble.*

*It's really great that you're trying to work things out with Georgette. It wouldn't surprise me at all if the two of you became good friends. I'm really looking forward to seeing her again—she's a nice kid, and cute, too.*

*I've got Halloween triple-circled in red on my calendar. There's no way I'm going to miss the Fox Hall party. If it's going to be a costume party, maybe I'll come dressed as Dracula. I vant to bite your neck!!!*

*Let me know what's going on.*

*Yours,*
*Sam*

"Wouldn't it be great if we coordinated our costumes with the guys'?" Palmer mused aloud. "Sam and I could be Romeo and Juliet."

"Or Beauty and the Beast. He'd be Beauty, of course," Amy teased.

Shanon released a small sigh. "I hope Lisa can make it.

It would be just perfect if all eight of us could get together."

"Ten," Amy corrected. "For sure, Maxie's going to invite Jose."

"I certainly hope so," Shanon said, her face brightening as she pulled out her latest letter from Mars.

*Dear Shanon,*

*Yours truly is the hit of Brighton General. I don't know if I've already mentioned it, but I'm doing some volunteer work there this semester. So far, it's going really well. Melanie, a little girl in the children's ward, was very depressed because her grandfather lives too far away to come see her. By coincidence, I happened to bump into a grouchy geezer on my way through the geriatrics wing. Turns out, he was acting so crabby because his daughter had just moved her kids to California. Before anyone could tell me not to, I wheeled the man over to Melanie's bed, and bingo—instant relatives! Now every oldster in the hospital wants to adopt one of the sick kids. I'd try sneaking in a few stray kittens and puppies as well, but I don't think the head nurse would go for it.*

*I wish finding a solution to the Lisa problem was as simple. Rob's pretty bummed out because she isn't communicating much with him either. He even sent her one of those fill-in-the-blanks letters, but she hasn't returned it yet.*

*Have you called Lisa? The way I see it, you haven't got anything to lose but this month's allowance. Make that half of this month's allowance—I'd be glad to invest a few bucks in a very good cause.*

*I know it's dumb to tell you not to worry, but I'll do it*

*anyway. With friends like you on her side, Lisa's sure to*
*make it through this.*

*Keep smiling,*
*Mars*

"What a fabulous idea!" Shanon squealed, scrambling to her feet. "Let's go call Lisa this very minute. We can use the pay phone in the snack bar." But as she fumbled through her pockets, her excitement faded fast. "Rats!" she moaned. "I forgot to bring my change purse."

"I don't have any money either," Amy said. Then, sliding a pointed glance in her roommate's direction, she added, "Of course we wouldn't need any money if one of us had a telephone credit card. Hint. Hint."

Palmer was dubious. "I promised my dad I wouldn't use it unless I absolutely had to."

"But this is a real emergency," Shanon pleaded.

"That's right. Lisa is our friend. We have to try to help her," Amy added.

Palmer looked from Amy's eager face to Shanon's and back again, then made her decision. "What are we waiting for?"

Less than five minutes later, the three Foxes were crowded into the phone booth. Palmer took care of business with the long distance operator, then handed the receiver to Shanon. "You talk to her first."

Shanon could hardly wait for the call to connect. After six long rings, a subdued "McGreevy residence" came over the line.

"Lisa, it's me—I mean us!" Shanon bubbled. "Since we didn't get a letter from you this week, we decided to reach out and touch you."

"Good to hear from you. How are things going?" Lisa's tone was dull, lifeless.

"Better than super. We want you to come to the Halloween party. All the guys will be there and—"

"Sounds nice," Lisa cut Shanon off. "But I don't think I'll be able to make it. I'm sure you'll have a great time, though."

"What's she saying?" Amy asked impatiently.

Shanon waved her to silence, now aware of a commotion at the other end. She caught the discordant sound of voices, and though she couldn't make out any specific words, the tone of the background conversation was clearly angry.

There was a pause, and then the sound was muffled, as if a hand had been clamped over the mouthpiece. After a few seconds, Lisa came back with, "Sorry about that. The television was turned up too loud."

"Is everything okay, Lisa?" Shanon asked.

"Peachy." The grim response was followed with, "I really appreciate your calling, but a couple of friends from school are due here any minute. We're going to the movies."

Shanon swallowed her disappointment. "Sounds like fun. Write us a letter when you have time."

"I will," Lisa said flatly before breaking the connection.

"What's going on?" Palmer demanded.

Shanon gently cradled the receiver, her forehead creased with worry. "Nothing good, I suspect. Lisa said the noise was coming from the TV, but I think her parents were having a fight."

"Poor Lisa," Amy exclaimed. "It must be awful for her."

"So much for family therapy. Lisa would've been better

64

off if her parents had stayed separated and sold their house. That way, at least she'd be here at Alma with us," Palmer said, glumly returning her credit card to her wallet. "She's stopped writing and she won't talk on the phone. What do we do now?"

Shanon's hazel eyes sparked with determination. "Build a fire and send up smoke signals, if necessary. Whether she knows it or not, Lisa McGreevy needs us; we'll just have to keep trying until we get through to her."

# CHAPTER 9

Dear Max,

It was a dumb idea for me to answer the ad you put in the Ardsley newspaper. I'm sure you expected a pen pal who was your own age. I won't be mad if you don't write to me again. Nobody's ever wanted to be bothered with me—why should you be any diferent?

Mr. and Mrs. Hurt let me stay with them because they're nice. I wish that they were really my folks, only I know that wouldn't work because I cause too much trouble. I'd like to change, but I don't know how.

Jose

Maxie cast a helpless glance across the room where the children were finger painting with Gina Hawkins, one of the other volunteers. Jose was crouched in a corner, watching from behind a chair he'd pulled up as a barricade. There was a sheet of paper on the floor in front of him, and from time to time, he marked it with a crayon.

His behavior gave Max the beginning of an idea. Ripping a blank page from her notebook, she hastily scribbled a reply.

*Dear Jose,*

*The only dumb idea you've had is trying to dump your pen pal. Whether you like it or not, you're stuck with me!*

*From now on, we'll use the bottom shelf of the bookcase for our mail drop. And if I don't find your answers to my letters there, I'LL COME LOOKING FOR YOU, TURKEY!*

Max printed the threat with so much pressure that the lead in her pencil broke. Fishing a pen from her purse, she added a smiling face, and then finished with a flourish:

*I've got a project in mind that would be lots of fun, but I'm going to need your help to pull it off. If you're interested, keep your antenna tuned to this station.*

*Love,*
*Max*

Folding the note in half, she sauntered casually past his hiding place and let it flutter from her fingers. When a quick glance assured her that the message was received, Max walked over to stand by Gina. "The kids are doing a fantastic job. These paintings are so good that everyone on campus should get a chance to see them. Why don't we put on an art show?" she suggested.

"What a great idea!" Gina exclaimed. "Alma's art students can frame the drawings, and we'll have refreshments at the opening. That's what they do in New York galleries."

"Sounds like fun," Max said happily. Facing the children, she asked, "Which of you little Picassos wants in on this? Raise your hands if—"

Max's speech was immediately drowned out by squeals of "Me! Me!" While Jose didn't move from his spot, Max thought she detected a flash of interest in his expression.

Encouraged, she shot the nine-year-old a bright smile. Then, turning back to Gina, she said, "I'll go run this by Mr. Griffith right now."

Max hurried from the room, stopping at the door for a quick peek back at the group. Jose was already heading toward the art table for some fresh paper and a supply of paints. He raised his head, meeting and then steadily holding her gaze. After a beat, the corners of his mouth lifted in a shy smile. It was a small victory, but Maxie couldn't have been prouder if she'd been handed the Nobel prize.

Minutes later Max was in the Grayson-Griffith apartment, enthusiastically outlining her idea to Dan Griffith. "Good thinking, Maxie," he said when she paused for breath. "Everyone will get a blue ribbon," he promised.

"Thanks," Max said, but she wasn't finished yet. Before she could stop herself, she blurted out, "Mr. G., if the Hurts love Jose so much, why don't they adopt him?"

Mr. Griffith gave her a long, searching look. "It's a complicated situation," he finally said. "The Hurts have no real claim on Jose. If the authorities found out that the Hurts are homeless and are keeping a child who doesn't belong to the family, Jose might be taken away from them altogether. Besides, they can't afford to hire a lawyer to take care of the procedures involved in legally adopting him," he explained. "Why do you ask?"

Not wanting to betray the trust Jose had given her, Max mumbled, "I was just wondering. It seemed like the logical thing for them to do."

"Mr. and Mrs. Hurt have always wanted the adoption. They haven't discussed it with Jose, though, because they don't want to raise his expectations. I don't think it would be a good idea for you to mention it to him either," he warned.

"I'd never do that," Maxie said solemnly.

The teacher accepted her assurance with a nod and, turning back to the shelf he was building, added an absent, "Things don't always go the way we think they should, but unfortunately that's the way the world turns."

*Unless someone gives it a little spin in another direction,* Maxie thought, hiding a smile.


"This is Brighton, not New Orleans. And besides, the Mardi Gras bit has been done a million times," Palmer squelched her stepsister's latest proposal for party decorations. Retrieving the elaborate sketches she had persuaded one of the girls in her art class to draw, she spread them out on the floor for inspection. "We'll use crepe paper streamers in a combination of Ardsley and Alma colors, and there will be blow-ups of the school shields on opposite walls."

Hands on her hips, Georgette marched past the line of drawings, the jut of her jaw every bit as stubborn as Palmer's. "In the first place, this is a costume party, so my Mardi Gras theme is much more appropriate than your Ardsley/Alma idea. And secondly, we want all of our guests to feel welcome. In case you've forgotten, your own pen pal Sam doesn't attend *either* school."

Palmer felt her cheeks flame—she *had* forgotten—but she quickly recovered her composure. "A lot you know. Sam used to go to Ardsley," she announced frostily. Then, turning to her suitemates for support, she said, "Be honest, guys—which of these presentations is better?"

Shanon and Amy had long since decided that neutrality was the best policy when it came to Durand vs. Durand. "Both are very nice," they replied in tactful unison.

"What do you think, Maxie?" Georgette asked.

But Max wasn't about to take sides either. "I think you're both missing the point," she said slyly. "Personally, I'd go with the traditional black and orange."

"Hmm," said Palmer thoughtfully. Since the suggestion hadn't come from her stepsister, she was more than willing to consider it. "It's hokey, but it *is* Halloween," she finally agreed.

"It would also be cheap," Amy pointed out. "Instead of buying the decorations, we could use piles of autumn leaves and dried corn stalks from the farm down the road."

Georgette's face brightened. "I'll ask my biology teacher if we can borrow the skeleton from the lab. With that and a few fake cobwebs, we can turn the foyer into a house of horrors."

"We could have a pumpkin-carving contest and hand out prizes for the scariest jack-o'-lantern," Shanon chipped in.

"All of this sounds good to me," Palmer gave the final okay. "By the way," she said, favoring Maxie with a gracious smile, "what did Jose say when you invited him to the party?"

"Nothing," Maxie responded, squirming. Still trying to

avoid an out-and-out lie, she added, "The Ardsley volunteers only come on Thursday."

"But you *are* going to ask him, aren't you?" Shanon persisted.

"Jose would probably be uncomfortable in a crowd of people. He's sort of shy." Glancing at her watch, Maxie faked dismay. "Oh, my gosh, I'm late! I was supposed to meet Gina in the studio ten minutes ago. We've got to nail down the details of the shelter kids' art exhibition."

Before the Foxes had a chance to ask any more questions, she snatched up her jacket and dashed from the room.

Palmer watched her go with a puzzled frown. "Max acts like she doesn't want Jose to come to the party," she said to the other girls. "I wonder why."

"If you ask me, Max is the one who's shy—not Jose," Shanon offered. "Maybe—"

"This is all very interesting," Georgette broke in, "but we really should get back to the matter at hand. In view of the party theme we've chosen, I think we should serve cranberry punch and pumpkin pie."

"That would be fine—if all our guests were dweebs," Palmer scoffed. "Don't you think apple cider and carrot cake would be more sophisticated, Shanon?"

"You'll have to settle this one without me. I've got to go to the *Ledger* office and do some proofreading," Shanon answered, beating a hasty path to the door.

Amy was only a step behind. "I'll walk you as far as the bookstore. I'm all out of loose-leaf paper."

As soon as they were safely out in the hallway, the two Foxes broke out laughing.

71

"With the double Durands in charge, it'll be a minor miracle if this Halloween party gets off the ground," Amy giggled.

"I just hope Suite 3-D is still in one piece when we get back."

As they strolled across the quadrangle, Amy turned serious. "I didn't want to mention this in front of Georgette, but the last time I wrote to John I asked him a few questions about Jose. I just got his answer today."

Shanon snapped to attention. "What did he say? Does John know Jose?"

Amy shook her head. "The only Jose who lives in Kirby Hall is a blond guy with green eyes."

"Maybe Max's Jose is in another dorm, or it could be that Jose is just his nickname."

"There's another possibility," Amy said hesitantly. "You know how uptight Max is about boys and dates, and we did push her hard about Paul. Do you think she could have invented the mystery mailman just to keep us off her back?"

"No way, Jose," Shanon responded, chuckling at the unintentional joke. "She's much too honest to do that. Speaking of which, sneaking around behind her back is giving me a giant case of the guilts. From now on, let's keep our noses out of Max's business."

"It's a deal," Amy agreed, turning off toward the bookstore with a cheery, "See you later."

Shanon's conscience felt considerably lighter as she walked into the *Ledger* office, and her spirits got a similar lift when she noticed the big smile on Kate Majors's face. "You look awfully happy," she said. "What's going on?"

"I just finished a computer link-up with Reggie," Kate

72

announced. And as Shanon's eyes lit up with interest, she added, "It was strictly business, of course." The older girl's cheeks warmed with a deep blush as she admitted, "Well, mostly."

As Shanon pulled up a chair beside the terminal station, she felt a knot form in the pit of her stomach.

"Did he say anything about Lisa? Is she okay?"

"He really isn't sure how Lisa is. She still isn't writing to him. But he's going home this weekend and he's got a plan," she assured Shanon. "Can you come in here early Saturday morning?"

Shanon eyed her friend curiously. "Sure. But why?"

"Reggie is going to call from the computer he's got set up in his bedroom. That way the charge will be billed to the McGreevys' number instead of *The Ledger*. As soon as the contact is made, he and I will do a fast fade and you'll go online with Lisa!"

Shanon's mouth dropped open. "That's incredible!" she cried happily. But almost instantly she was hit by a wave of doubt. "Suppose she won't talk to me?"

"She will. In fact, Reggie thinks you're the only one who can get through to her."

"I'll do my best," Shanon promised, giving the other girl a big hug. "Thanks a lot, Kate. I owe you for this one."

"Glad to help." The usually solemn editor grinned mischievously, finishing, "But if you're really into gratitude, I'll let you do all my proofreading for the rest of the term."

# CHAPTER 10

"It's all yours," Kate said after she had read Reggie's short message establishing the computer link. Giving Shanon's shoulder an encouraging pat, the editor tactfully retreated to the other side of the room.

Shanon stared at the flickering cursor on the computer screen, her palms clammy. All the snappy beginnings she had rehearsed on the way to the *Ledger* office had vanished from her brain, so she simply typed:

HI, LISA.

When nothing else came to mind, she added /GA, the computer symbol for "go ahead." After what seemed like a thousand years a question finally flashed onto the screen.

WHAT'S UP? /GA

She keyed in OKAY to let Lisa know the message had been received, then added, THAT'S WHAT I'D LIKE TO KNOW! I'M SUPPOSED TO BE YOUR BEST FRIEND, YOU DOPE—TALK TO ME!!!!!/GA

For a moment, Shanon thought she had pushed too hard, but then a response came back:

OKAY. I REALLY SCREWED UP THIS TIME./GA

"This is like pulling teeth," Shanon thought, but she was determined to find out what was really troubling Lisa. OKAY, she shot back. WHAT DID YOU DO?/GA

OKAY. MISSION "KEEP FAMILY TOGETHER" IS A TOTAL BUST. I'M LIVING IN THE MIDDLE OF WORLD WAR III. MOM AND DAD DON'T EVEN TRY TO HIDE THEIR ARGUMENTS FROM ME ANYMORE.

The words were now coming so fast that Shanon could scarcely keep up with them:

IF I HAD GONE BACK TO ALMA, REGGIE WOULDN'T BE MAD AT ME. HE ALWAYS SAID WE HAD TO LET MOM AND DAD WORK THINGS OUT IN THEIR OWN WAY. I SHOULD HAVE LISTENED TO HIM./GA

Shanon knew there was nothing she could do to help Lisa come to terms with her parents' problems, but she could clear up one misunderstanding.

OKAY, she typed in. TALK TO REGGIE A.S.A.P. HE THINKS YOU'RE THE ONE WHO'S MAD BECAUSE HE LEFT YOU TO DEAL WITH THE PROBLEM BY YOURSELF./GA

OKAY. OKAY, OKAY, OKAY!! BOY, IS THAT A RELIEF!!!/GA

OKAY. ORDER NUMBER TWO IS, WRITE TO ROB! HE MISSES YOUR LETTERS./GA

OKAY. I MISS HIM ALMOST AS MUCH AS I MISS YOU, SHANON. HAVE I TOLD YOU LATELY THAT YOU'RE MY BEST FRIEND?/GA

OKAY. I KNOW. I FEEL THE SAME WAY ABOUT YOU. REMIND ME TO TELL YOU ABOUT THE CHAT WE HAD IN THE SWIMMING POOL./GA

OKAY. SAY WHAT??????/GA

OKAY. YOU REALLY HAD TO BE THERE. I'LL WRITE SOON./GA

OKAY. IT'S EASIER FOR ME TO TALK THIS WAY. CAN WE GET ONLINE AGAIN NEXT SATURDAY?/GA

OKAY. TERRIFIC! WILL YOUR PARENTS MIND ABOUT THE MONEY? IF SO, I'LL CHIP IN HALF THE COST. BYE, NOW. LOVE YA./GA

Shanon clicked off the computer, feeling better than she had since the school term began.

75

"Is everything straightened out?" Kate asked, returning to her desk.

"Not yet, but at least we made a start," Shanon replied happily.

"Good. Now maybe we can get back to the business of running this newspaper," the editor-in-chief said briskly. "We need a lead story for the next issue. Something meaty, but not too heavy."

"Maxie's art exhibit!" Shanon exclaimed. And by the time she'd finished describing the upcoming shelter children's art show, Kate had caught some of her enthusiasm.

"Pure human interest," Kate said approvingly. "You write the story and I'll take the photographs."

"I can't wait to tell Max about this. She's going to be so excited!"

"You look uptight. Are you okay?" Gina Hawkins asked as she selected a fudgy square from the tray Maxie was holding.

"I've still got a pulse—I think," Max quipped, her gaze skidding over the main hall of the Meeting House. Alma students and faculty mingled in appreciative clusters around the children's work. She shifted uncomfortably, wishing she'd chosen a conservative dress instead of the oversized chartreuse sweater and short leather skirt that topped her silver cowboy boots.

"Isn't this a fantastic crowd? I'd better check to see if we have enough refreshments," Gina said, hurrying away.

"There's enough punch and brownies in the kitchen to feed the whole state of New Hampshire," Max called after her.

76

"Hold that pose and say cheese," Kate Majors commanded, striding up with her camera.

Maxie shielded her eyes from the sudden flash. "Be careful when you photograph the kids. Some of them are really shy," she warned, thinking mostly of Jose.

"Don't be silly, they love it." Kate adjusted her lens and bounced off toward the podium, where Miss Pryn was waiting to hand out the ribbons.

As she looked around the crowded room, Maxie felt a nervous flutter in her stomach. She hadn't realized that the event would attract so much attention. And she certainly hadn't expected her suitemates to make such a big deal about it. But they'd all insisted they wouldn't miss the show for anything. Palmer had spent hours in front of the mirror, rejecting a dozen blouses before settling on a lavender one which went with the silk scarf her stepmother had painted for her.

As the trio of Foxes made their way through the crowd, Max suddenly wondered how on earth she was going to keep them from learning Jose's true identity.

"You've done a terrific job coordinating all of this, Max," Amy said, plucking a brownie from the tray.

"Fabulous," Palmer seconded. She adjusted a fold of the butterfly scarf draped over her shoulder and, scanning the crush around them, said pointedly, "Have any of the boy volunteers shown up yet?"

"This is just an Alma thing. We didn't have time to spread the word to Ardsley," Max explained.

"That's too bad," Shanon said, clearly disappointed. "We were hoping we'd get to meet Jose."

Maxie allowed herself an inward groan. She realized

77

that she should have stopped the mystery mailman game way before now. If anything happened to blow her cover, she'd be in for a lot of teasing. "Well, he—"

"There's Mr. Griffith and that weirdo kid who hangs out with him," Amy interjected, pointing to a spot near the center of the exhibit.

Maxie turned around slowly. Jose and the teacher were standing beside a cloth-draped easel. "He isn't a weirdo, he's just bashful," she defended her secret pen pal.

"He looks a lot better than he did the last time I saw him. With his hair slicked down and that suit on, he's really very cute." Shanon smoothed her pleated skirt, studying the scene intently. "Did he paint a picture for the show?"

A shadow of disappointment slid across Maxie's features. "I really thought he might, but Gina and I couldn't find his entry when we were setting up," she said. "We—" She broke off as a sudden movement across the room caught her eye. It was Mr. Griffith, waving vigorously.

Amy returned the salute. "I think Mr. G. wants us over there."

"You guys stay put. I'll go see what's up," Maxie said. Handing Palmer the cookie tray with a terse "Hold this," she headed off across the room.

After Palmer, Amy, and Shanon had helped themselves to the last of the brownies, the three girls tagged along behind.

"We've got a surprise for you, Ms. Schloss," Mr. Griffith announced when all the Foxes were clustered around the covered easel. But before he could reveal it, Gina dashed up to claim his attention. "Excuse me, Mr. Griffith, but Miss Pryn wants to speak with you."

"Duty calls," he said, giving Jose's shoulder a pat. "You can handle it, Jose."

As the teacher moved away, the little boy turned an anxious glance toward Maxie.

She smiled her encouragement. Taking a deep breath, Jose yanked the drape from the painting on the easel.

For a timeless moment, all Maxie could do was stare. The subject was a dark tornado with angry lightning bolts forking through its center. But the surrounding sky was a serene blue, and a glorious rainbow arched protectively over the storm. At the bottom in large block letters was the inscription, "For Maxie, from Jose."

"It's wonderful," she murmured, deeply moved. Oblivious to the rest of the onlookers, she held out her hand. "This is the nicest thing anyone's ever done for me. Thank you so much, Jose."

He gazed at her mutely, his fingers gripping hers tightly.

A trio of gasps from behind spun Maxie around. The Foxes were wide-eyed with shock. The empty tray slipped from Palmer's hands, clattering noisily against the hardwood floor. Just then, Kate arrived on the scene with her camera, clicking and flashing away.

Maxie's first thought was to get Jose away from the hubbub. She had no idea what her suitemates were liable to say, and she didn't want to risk having him hurt or embarrassed.

"I'm not the only klutz in 3-D," she said with a forced chuckle as she retrieved the tray. Handing it to the boy, she requested, "Please take this back to the kitchen for me, Jose."

Amy watched him disappear into the crowd, her mouth opening and closing a few times before she could get out a strangled, "Jose?"

"Let me get this straight. That's the mystery mailman?" Shanon blurted out incredulously.

A rush of color zipped up Maxie's neck. Her secret was out. "Yep," she admitted, turning even redder. "All four feet two inches of him. I tried to tell you the day I found out who he was, but nobody would listen."

Palmer clapped a hand over her mouth, but not in time to catch a hoot of hilarity.

Shanon pursed her lips in a vain attempt to keep a straight face. "You've had plenty of chances to come clean since then."

The flush on Max's face raced clear up to her hairline. "I know, but everyone was having such a good time thinking he was a tall, dark, handsome Ardie. I didn't want to spoil the fun," she mumbled lamely.

"I can see why you didn't want to invite him to the Halloween party," Palmer gasped, nearly doubled over with laughter. "You'd be the only girl in Fox Hall whose date still needed a baby-sitter!"

"Knock it off, Palm. . . ." The rest of Amy's warning dissolved in a helpless burst of giggles.

Usually sensitive Shanon did her best to resist the silliness, but it was a losing battle and she joined in the laughter.

"Cut it out, guys," Maxie snapped, her humiliation overshadowed by a rising tide of anger.

The merriment abruptly ceased, but not because of her fiery command. Now shamefaced and sober, the other girls stared past Maxie. When she turned to follow the direction of their gazes, her heart sank to the soles of her cowboy boots. Jose Hurt was standing directly behind her.

It was obvious the child had overheard the whole conversation. His face was pale and his eyes were filled with pain.

"Jose, I . . . ." The rest of the sentence stuck in Maxie's throat. She took a step toward him, extending her hand.

Features hardened into a mask of sullenness, he spun on his heel and ran off through the crowd.

"I'm so sorry, Max," Shanon said humbly.

"That's right," Palmer chimed in. "We didn't mean to hurt your feelings."

Maxie's eyes flashed green fire. "*My* feelings!?" she echoed furiously. "Who cares about *my* feelings? It's Jose's feelings that I'm worried about. Imagine how that poor little kid must feel now!"

"We didn't see him standing there until it was too late," Amy said, awkwardly patting Maxie's arm.

Max jerked away from the touch. "I don't have time to listen to your excuses," she snapped. "I've got to go straighten out the mess we've made—if I can," she added, hurrying off after the boy.

But by the time she got through the crush of people and out into the hallway, there was no sign of Jose. Thinking he might have run outside, she started a thorough search of the grounds around the Meeting House. Half an hour went by before she finally admitted defeat.

Mr. Griffith met her as she was coming back into the building. "The other girls told me what happened. Did you find Jose?" he asked.

She just shook her head, unable to put her misery into words.

"He's bound to be around here somewhere. I'll have a talk with him." The teacher gave her shoulder a comforting squeeze, adding, "Gina and I can handle the rest of the show. Why don't you go on back to the dorm?"

Maxie started off with a deep sigh, but halfway down the front walk she turned back again. There was still one more place she had to search.

Though the room where she'd discovered her pen pal's true identity was deserted, his presence seemed to linger in every corner. She searched all his favorite hiding places with no success. Her last hope was the bookcase that had served as their mailbox.

"Please let that be from Jose," she whispered when she spotted an envelope peeking out from between two over-sized picturebooks. Heart pounding, she pulled out a wrinkled sheet of notebook paper.

*Dear Max,*
*It's all my fault that your friends laughed at you. I'm sorry for the trouble I caused. This is the last time I'll ever write to you, but I'll always remember all the nice things you did for me.*

*Good-bye forever,*
*Jose Hurt*
*P.S. I hope you liked the picture. In case you didn't know, you are the rainbow.*

# CHAPTER 11

———◆———

Dear Mars,

When I wrote you about the mess the Foxes made at the children's art exhibition, I didn't know how bad things were going to get. Max went back to the shelter to talk to Jose, but he was gone. His foster family moved out of there that same night because Mr. Hurt found work and a new place for them to live. Mrs. Hurt left a note saying how much she appreciated all that Max had done for the children. Max never got to say good-bye to Jose, though.

Amy, Palmer, and I all feel really terrible about this, and we've decided to run a special ad in The Ledger and The Lion. If Jose is still reading the school newspapers, maybe he'll respond.

Let me know right away if you think of anything else we can do.

Yours always,
Shanon

Dear Sam,

Max still won't talk to me, and I can't really blame her.

It was mean and stupid of me to tease her so hard about Jose. More and more I'm finding out what a special person she is. Mr. Griffith was amazed when he learned that Jose had been writing to her. The kid has never opened up like that with anyone else.

The family didn't leave a forwarding address, but we do know that Mr. Hurt is now working in an orchard somewhere close by. Trouble is, there are half a dozen apple farms just outside of Brighton, and we have no idea which is the right one. I know that one of the members of your band has a car and a driver's license, and I'd be glad to pay for the gas if you guys would check out all the orchards. If you can locate Jose, you'll be the most honored V.I.P. at the Halloween party.

Speaking of October 31st, I've decided to dress up as Cleopatra. I called the rental shop in Brighton, and they're holding a costume for me. It would be terrific if someone special I know would come as Marc Anthony—HINT, HINT!!!

Love,
Palmer

Dear John,

I don't have another verse for our rap song, but I'm seriously in need of help from Captain Fixit. From what we've been able to piece together about Jose's background, we think that a lot of his problems have to do with feeling that he doesn't really belong to a family. The Hurts can't even be his official foster parents because they're temporarily homeless. They need someone to help them with the legal mumbo-jumbo.

That's where you come in. Since your dad is a lawyer,

*would you ask him if he knows a way to cut through the red tape? Shanon and Palmer are in on this, too, but we're not telling Maxie about any of it just yet. It would be awful to get her hopes up if we can't deliver.*

*Thanks loads, pal. Write back as soon as possible.*

*Best,*
*Amy*

AD FOR THE PERSONALS COLUMN OF THE ALMA LEDGER AND ARDSLEY LION:

*Dear Jose,*
*Please accept this apology for our behavior at the Alma art show. We may be older than you, but we're certainly not as wise. We know now that a pen pal's age doesn't matter. It's what's in his head and heart that really counts.*

*Maxie misses your letters very much. She is our friend, and it hurts us to see how sad she is. Please write to her very soon.*

*We hope you can forgive us, because we would like to become your pen pals, too.*

*Very, very, very sincerely,*
*Shanon Davis*
*Amy Ho*
*Palmer Durand*

"We're ordering pizzas from Figaro's. What do you want on yours, Max?" Shanon asked from the doorway of their bedroom.

"Nothing. I'm not hungry," Maxie answered, not looking up from her history book.

"Palmer's treat," Shanon persisted. "She won the argu-

85

ment she and Georgette had over the guest list for the party, and she wants to celebrate."

"That's nice."

Shanon's breath came out in a dispirited sigh. "We've all said we're sorry a hundred times. Aren't you ever going to stop being mad?"

"I'm not mad. I just want to be alone."

"Suit yourself. We're ordering a super-Monstro with double pepperoni and mushrooms. If you change your mind, we can share it." With that offer, Shanon gently shut the door behind her and trudged into the sitting room.

After a moment, Maxie closed her book and leaned back against the pillow. She had reread the same page ten times, and she still didn't have the foggiest notion what was on it. Staring up at the ceiling, she let her mind wander.

The truth was, her anger at her suitemates had long since ebbed away. A lot of soul-searching had convinced her that they weren't totally at fault for the Jose Hurt disaster. But it would take a lot of courage to admit her share of the blame.

"Do it now, you chicken," she scolded herself aloud. And swinging her long legs over the side of the bed, she stood up and marched out into the sitting room.

"If you interrupt me, I'm going to lose my nerve. So everybody keep quiet until I'm finished," she announced, eyes firmly focused a few inches over their heads.

There was dead silence in the room.

"Number one, I'm sorry. I've been acting like a total dweeb. If I had told you the truth in the beginning, you would never have made those jokes about Jose at the show. In fact, I bet you would have done your best to help me get through to him." Still avoiding their eyes, she swallowed hard and pushed on. "Number two, I've decided to answer Paul Grant's letter. It won't be the same as writing to Jose, but at least I'll be part of the gang again."

"Are you finished?" Amy asked softly.

Max nodded.

"Good. I hate long, sappy speeches," Palmer said, bouncing up from the loveseat to grab Maxie's hand. "You don't have to have a pen pal if you don't want one, you big klutz."

"We wouldn't care if you never wrote another letter in your entire life." Shanon took Max's other hand, finishing, "We've really missed sharing things with you."

"Now close your eyes," Amy instructed. "We're going to lead you to a surprise."

Maxie obeyed, relieved and happier than she'd been all week.

After a few stumbling paces, Palmer said, "You can look now."

Max found herself facing the outside wall of the sitting room. The cherished space that had once held Lisa's favorite poster was no longer empty. Her suitemates had filled it with Jose's painting.

"We accidentally found the last letter he wrote you. We know how sad you've been, and we thought this might help," Amy said.

Palmer flashed a smug grin. "It was my idea."

Maxie tried for a corny joke to hide her emotion, but all that came out was a shaky, "Thanks a lot, guys."

"Now that that's over, we're going to order the pizza," Palmer said, dragging Amy toward the door.

"Jose was right," Shanon said, slipping her arm around Maxie's waist. "You really are a rainbow."

# CHAPTER 12

---

Eight days before the 31st and counting, Project Halloween Party was nearing lift-off. The Fox Hall common room was in pre-party disarray, with bundles of dried corn stalks piled up by the door, rolls of black and orange crepe paper waiting to be twisted into streamers. Mr. Bones, the biology department's contribution, hung in a far corner, grinning his ghastly approval.

The social committee was functioning fairly smoothly— a minor miracle, considering the two co-chairpersons. The Durands' current disagreement was over what music to play on the big night.

"Paula Abdul for sure, and of course New Kids," Georgette decided, removing two CDs from the stack she had collected from the girls on her floor. After a second hesitation, she added a Beach Boys album. "I thought it might be fun if we mixed in a few oldies."

"Ugh!" Palmer quickly vetoed Georgette's third selection. "Where in the world did you find that relic?"

"I brought it from home. Dad and I used to listen to it

all the time. The Beach Boys are one of his favorite groups," Georgette informed her stepsister.

"I knew that," Palmer snapped.

"Dan and Maggie would probably love a stroll down memory lane," Maxie intervened before the discussion could escalate into a full-scale argument. "We'll play the Beach Boys for them during the jack-o'-lantern carving contest."

"Maybe we can persuade the Griffiths to put on an exhibition of the old dances," Georgette suggested eagerly.

"That's not a bad idea," Palmer said with grudging admiration. "Records are okay, but it would be really great if we could have some live entertainment."

"Why don't you ask Sam if he and his band could play," her stepsister piped up.

"Yeah, Palmer. That would be neat," Maxie joined in.

Palmer toyed with the idea for a minute, then shook her head. "It wouldn't be fair to him. Music is a serious business for Sam, and if he had to work, he would have less time to enjoy himself." What she really meant was that he would have less time to spend with her, but she wasn't about to tell that to Georgette.

Her stepsister shot her an exasperated look. "That's very considerate, but I'm sure Sam would love—"

"I'm not asking him. Period—exclamation point—end of discussion," Palmer said stubbornly.

Maxie sighed inwardly, then changed the subject. "Have you decided on a costume, Georgette?"

The younger girl nodded happily. "I can't tell you what it is, though. I want it to be a surprise. What are you wearing, Sis?"

"A Maid Marian costume. Sam is coming as my Robin Hood," Palmer fibbed.

Shanon and Amy turned questioning eyes on Palmer, but she refused to meet their gaze.

"Surprise, surprise—I'm going to be a clown," Max broke the awkward silence. Then, once again she changed the subject. "We'd better move on to the invitations. I've finished the guest list, so one of us can start addressing the envelopes."

"I'll do it," Georgette volunteered.

"My handwriting's better," Palmer insisted.

Each grasped a side of the guest list.

Before they could rip it in two, Shanon dashed up to the table with a breathless, "Can you come out to the lobby for a minute, Palmer?"

"I'm right in the middle of—"

"Amy and I need to talk to you about"—Shanon stopped abruptly, angling an oblique glance toward Maxie before she finished—"the project Sam and John are working on."

Palmer's eyes lit up and she released her half of the list with a gracious, "Knock yourself out, Georgette."

A puzzled Maxie watched her suitemates rush from the room. It wasn't at all like Palmer to give in so easily.

"Are you positive this is the correct address for Palmer's pen pal?" Georgette broke into Maxie's train of thought.

"It must be. She wrote it on the list herself," Maxie assured her. "Why do you ask?"

"Just double-checking," Georgette answered innocently. "Palmer would be very upset if Sam's invitation got sent to the wrong place."

But invitations were the last thing on Palmer's mind as

she and Shanon hurried toward the mailboxes in Booth Hall.

"Here's the latest from John!" Amy reported, and immediately began reading it out loud:

*Dear Amy,*
> *he's a klutzy goof who's forever in a stew,*
*but he's got good connections, and they know what to do*
> *captain fixit—captain fixit*
*he's the ever-lovin' pen pal who came through for you!*

*In other words . . . my dad hooked me up with an attorney who went to law school with him and who now has an office in Brighton. His name is Kenneth Burke, and when I phoned him, he seemed very interested in Jose's case.*

*This is the best part: Mr. Burke has got major dollars and a social conscience, so he does a lot of Pro Bono work. (In case you don't know, that's legalese for free!)*

*He's not promising results, but he is willing to talk to the Hurts. Although it'll probably be a long time before they can adopt Jose, Mr. Burke thinks he might be able to convince the Social Services Department that Jose should stay with the family.*

> *Your pal,*
> *John*

"I knew John would come through!" Amy squealed.

"Let's not celebrate just yet," Shanon warned. "Mr.

Burke can't talk to the Hurts if we can't find them."

"Wait a minute," Palmer said. "There's a letter in my box, too. From Sam!" she cried, pulling the envelope from her slot. "Maybe *he* has some news about the Hurts." The other girls gathered around as she impatiently tore it open.

*Dear Palmer,*

*You owe me $10.83 for gas—and a hug for determination. We had to go to five orchards before we hit pay dirt. The Hurts are living in an employees' trailer park at Ferguson's Fruit Farm, and the address is Route 7, Box 328, Brighton.*

*I didn't see Jose, but I left the copy of* The Ledger *you sent with his mother. I'm sure she can get him to read the letter you, Amy, and Shanon ran in the Personals column.*

> *Stay sweet,*
> *Sam*

*P.S. I'll collect the second part of my bill on Halloween.*

While Palmer reread the P.S. with a satisfied smile, Amy let out a triumphant whoop.

"We've got all the pieces, but we're going to need some help putting them together," cautious Shanon said. "We don't even know Mr. and Mrs. Hurt. And even though Sam's met them, he can't just waltz over and say we've found them a lawyer."

Amy's expression turned solemn. "You have a point. We're right back to square one unless we find a good middleman."

"Someone tactful and persuasive, who already knows the family," Palmer concluded.

"How's it going, girls?" Mr. Griffith called out as he passed them by, Gracie's leash in one hand and a fistful of mail in the other.

Without a word, the three Foxes took off after him.

# CHAPTER 13

Saturday morning at 9:00 sharp, Shanon was back at the *Ledger* office, "talking" to Lisa via the computer.

...OKAY. I CAN'T MAKE IT TO THE PARTY. MY GRANDMOTHER POPPED IN YESTERDAY. (THE LAST TIME GAMMY PAID ONE OF HER "SHORT" VISITS, SHE ARRIVED ON THE FOURTH OF JULY AND LEFT NEW YEAR'S DAY!) SOMETHING TELLS ME THIS IS GOING TO BE A VERY HAIRY HALLOWEEN./GA

Shanon grinned as she typed: OKAY. WHY?/GA

OKAY. MOM AND DAD HAVEN'T TOLD HER THEY'RE HAVING PROBLEMS. THEY'RE ACTING AS THOUGH EVERYTHING IS PEACHY KEEN. I'M SURE GAMMY'S WISE TO THE WHOLE DEAL, BUT SHE'S PRETENDING, TOO./GA

OKAY. HOW ABOUT YOU?/GA

OKAY. I'M GOING ALONG WITH THE PROGRAM, AND MY SMILE MUSCLES ARE CRACKING UNDER THE STRAIN. ENOUGH OF THIS NONSENSE, THOUGH. WHAT KIND OF COSTUME ARE YOU WEARING TO THE HALLOWEEN PARTY?

OKAY. I'M DRESSING AS AN ALIEN FROM THE PLANET DELTA THREE. MARS WILL BE COMING AS A MARTIAN, OF COURSE. SPEAKING OF COSTUMES, PALMER IS PICKING HERS UP THIS AFTERNOON. SHE'S GOING TO BE CLEOPATRA. AMY, MAXIE, AND I ARE TAGGING ALONG./GA

OKAY. HAVE FUN, AND IF YOU STOP BY FIGARO'S, EAT A MONSTRO FOR ME./GA

OKAY. LISA— Shanon lifted her hands from the keyboard for a moment. She wasn't sure the advice she was about to offer was right, but she flexed her fingers and went ahead with it anyway.

IF I WERE YOU, I'D HAVE A TALK WITH YOUR GRANDMOTHER. SHE MIGHT BE ABLE TO HELP YOU GET OPERATION "FAMILY TOGETHERNESS" BACK ON TRACK. BYE, NOW—LUV YA.

A few hours later, the girls entered Clyde's Custom Costumes.

"Here's your costume, Ms. Durand," the owner grumped. He reluctantly pushed a large cardboard box across the counter toward Palmer. "It's in mint condition now, so if there are any spots, tears, rips, stains, or other damage when you return it, you will be held responsible."

"I assure you I know how to take care of clothes," Palmer shot back haughtily. She tilted her head to read the label on the side. "Hold up, Mr. Clyde, you've made a mistake. I reserved a Cleopatra costume, and this one's a Maid Marian."

"Cleopatra?" Maxie stared at Palmer in surprise. "I thought you told Georgette you were dressing as Maid Marian."

"I just said that to throw her off. The less she knows about my business, the better I like it," Palmer insisted.

The proprietor peered at the box, then turned to shuffle toward the rear of the store, muttering and snorting as he went.

While Amy, Max, and Palmer impatiently waited for him to return, Shanon's attention was drawn to a nearby rack of headbands. The one she selected had two long springs attached to the top, each sprouting a lash-fringed,

95

bloodshot eyeball. "Wouldn't this be the perfect finishing touch for my alien outfit?" she asked, trying it on for her friends' approval.

"Go for it," Amy urged.

"I've already spent the last of my allowance," Shanon said, returning the silly ornament to the rack.

Palmer riffled through the thin sheaf of bills in her wallet, her face concerned. "I'd offer to lend you the money, but I've barely got enough to cover my rental fee."

Maxie grinned. "You could always use your fantastic plastic."

"My fantastic plastic is grounded this month. Dad's decided it's time I learned to stick to a budget." Palmer fingered the package on the counter, her blue eyes flashing angrily. "Of course, Goody-Goody Georgette never gets anywhere near her limit. It would serve her right if I added my charges to her bill."

"That would be really sneaky," Shanon protested.

"It's also illegal—which is the main reason I'm not going to try it," Palmer said.

Clyde's reappearance cut short the conversation. He shambled back to the counter, waving a sales ticket under Palmer's nose. "There's no mistake. You get the Maid Marian special," he informed her. "A Miss Georgette Durand came in this morning and authorized the switch."

"She had no right to do that," Palmer said indignantly. "It's *my* costume!"

"You'll have to work that out with her," Clyde said. "By the way, the other Miss Durand took care of your security deposit and rental fee when she charged her own costume." The man pinned Palmer with a disapproving scowl and handed her a slip of paper. "She also left this message for you."

*Surprise, big sister!*
*I hope you won't be offended because I paid without asking you first. It's my way of saying I'm sorry for the disagreements we've had.*

*Love,*
*Georgette*

P.S. *I'm glad I was able to straighten out the misunderstanding before it was too late. They apparently got your order mixed up with someone else's. Luckily, they still had one Maid Marian left. I know you're going to look great in it.*

"She was trying to help," Amy murmured.

"It was generous, too," Shanon added.

If there had been a guilt meter handy, Palmer's reading would have zoomed right off the dial. "Okay, okay, it was a sweet gesture. But I still want the Cleopatra costume," she insisted.

"It's already been rented out, and I don't have another one in stock," Clyde told her. "In fact, this Maid Marian and a gorilla suit are all I have left in your size. Which one do you want?"

Palmer snatched the box off the counter and hurried from the store. But out on the sidewalk, her steps slowed. Halfway down the block she came to an abrupt halt. "I feel like a total rat," she announced remorsefully. "I've been acting really mean, spiteful, and jealous—all the things I accused Georgette of."

"Well, she *has* needled you once or twice," Shanon said judiciously.

"But I'm older. It's up to me to set a good example." And with that, Palmer dumped the box into Amy's arms and ran back to the store. She returned a few minutes later to hand Shanon a brown paper bag. "It's your alien headband."

"Thanks, but you didn't have to do that," Shanon protested.

"Yes, I did." Palmer arranged her features in a pious expression, clasping her hands together. "You're looking at the new Palmer Durand. From now on, I'm going to be kind and generous. You can all borrow my clothes anytime you like."

Maxie slid her a sly look. "Even your new blue cashmere sweater?"

Palmer gulped. "Well. . . ."

"You don't have to go overboard with this," Amy said wryly. "I don't think I could take rooming with a saint."

Palmer practically glowed with righteousness all the way back to the dorm. The aura was almost visible by the time she spotted Georgette waiting by the door to 3-D, costume box in hand. "Thank you so much. You practically saved my life!" she breathed, clasping her stepsister in a warm hug.

"No problem," Georgette responded, beaming. "Dad keeps telling me it's unnatural for a girl my age to spend so little money. I'm sure he'll be delighted to get the bill."

"How delightful for you both," Palmer said, quickly dropping her arms to her sides.

"Would you like to come in and visit, Georgette?" Shanon invited. "We're all going to work on our outfits."

"I thought you'd never ask. If you don't mind, I'd like to try on my costume so you can tell me if it looks okay," she said, following the others into the suite.

Palmer set her box down on the loveseat, eyes gleaming as she began ripping off the tape. "I was going to save the big unveiling for the night of the party, but I can't wait."

"Me neither," Georgette said. "Can I change in one of the bedrooms? I want to make a grand entrance."

"Sure," Maxie said. "Use mine."

It took Palmer less than a minute to slip into the full-skirted, velvet gown of the Maid Marian costume. The snug bodice was pointed into a vee that emphasized the slenderness of her waist, and the rich forest green color set off her rosy skin and pale blond hair. "Somebody help me with this headdress," she requested.

As Shanon settled the tall, satin cone in place, the chiffon attached to its peak swirled around Palmer's shoulders like a filmy cloud.

"It's absolutely fabulous," Amy declared.

"Gorgeous," Shanon agreed. "Sam's not going to know what hit him."

"But it's all wrong, because he's coming as Marc Anthony," Palmer pouted.

"It's your own fault," Maxie pointed out, hiding a smile. "If you hadn't lied to Georgette, she wouldn't have had Mr. Clyde switch the costumes."

"It's a lot more glamorous than a gorilla suit," Amy added with a giggle.

Palmer frowned. "I'd still like to get my hands on the person who rented my Cleopatra costume. I wish I knew who in the world it was."

Maxie's mouth suddenly dropped open, but nothing came out. Her eyes widened in amazement as she stared past Palmer.

"Ta-da!" Georgette trumpeted from behind. "I had to pay extra to have the skirt shortened, but I think it was worth the expense."

The creamy pleats of her gown swirled in graceful folds about her ankles, and the jewel-encrusted necklace looked like one of the pieces from the King Tut collection. Arranging her elaborate crown so that its golden lotus flower graced the center of her forehead, Georgette gazed at them expectantly. "So, how do you like my Cleopatra costume?"

"Oh, boy," Amy mumbled, sagging down on the loveseat.

Not wanting to be in the line of fire, Shanon took a few backward steps. "Remember, this is the new Palmer Durand," she cautioned Maid Marian.

It took Palmer's last atom of self-control to keep from shrieking, but she managed it. "Why did you pick that costume?" she asked, her tone deadly calm.

"Mr. Clyde was so sweet when I told him what a terrible mistake he'd made, and I thought it would save him trouble if I rented the Cleopatra," Georgette explained. When there was no response from Palmer, her stepsister's eagerness faded into puzzled dismay. "You aren't angry with me, are you?"

Palmer swallowed hard. She couldn't very well admit to the lie she'd told. "Of course not," she said stiffly. "You did me a big favor. And anyway, the Cleopatra dress would've been all wrong for me. That off-white shade makes blondes look washed out."

As soon as the words left her lips, she realized her blunder: Georgette's coloring was identical to her own.

"I'll try to return the outfit tomorrow," Georgette sighed, her small face forlorn. She removed her crown and laid it carefully on the loveseat. "I wish I had your flair for dressing, Palmer. You've got the best taste of anybody I know."

There was an appealing ring of sincerity in Georgette's voice, and Palmer couldn't resist the compliment. "You'll make a beautiful Cleopatra, but you should do something different with your hair," she said, walking over to finger Georgette's curls. "Egyptian women in the queen's time wore lots of braids in their hair."

"My roommate Tina is a whiz at braids. I'm sure I can get her to do mine."

"We could probably find a book of authentic styles in the library," Palmer added, getting caught up in the plan.

"And I'll use lots of mascara," Georgette proposed.

"Heavy eyeliner, too. I picked up a new one last week in Brighton. Let's go try it on."

Linking hands, the Durand sisters walked toward the bedroom, chattering happily about clothes and cosmetics.

"What just happened here?" Amy asked when the two were out of earshot.

"I saw it, but I don't believe it," Shanon gasped. "This must really be a new Palmer Durand. The old one would've killed Georgette."

Maxie's expression was dubious. "Do you really think this is going to last?"

"Peace is breaking out all over, these days," said Shanon, ever the optimist. "After all, they tore down the Berlin Wall, didn't they?"

101

# CHAPTER 14

The Foxes of the Third Dimension WANT YOU at the FOX HALL HALLOWEEN PARTY!

WE DARE YOU TO COME!

"One of your eyebrows is crooked," Amy said, peering into the mirror at her suitemate's nearly finished clown face.

Maxie redrew the lines of the triangle over her left eye, then attached a red plastic ball to the tip of her nose. "How's that?" she asked, mugging at her reflection.

"Goofy," Amy giggled, "but great. What are you going to do with your hair?"

"Hide most of it." Maxie tugged on a white rubber cap, fluffing the auburn curls that poked out at the edges. From a distance, it appeared as though the top of her head was completely bald.

Amy was impressed by the transformation. "You're a real pro," she marveled.

"I've had lots of practice. I'm always a clown on Halloween."

"And every other day of the year," Amy teased, playfully tweaking the gigantic, polka-dotted bow tie under Maxie's chin. "But, seriously, don't you ever get tired of wearing the same costume?"

"I switched once. When I was ten, I went to my first boy-girl party dressed as a fairy princess," Max admitted, cringing at the memory. "Leonard Figley asked me to dance, and I was so nervous I poked him in the mouth with my magic wand. The star on the tip got caught in his braces."

"Oh, no!" Amy groaned.

"It gets worse. When I yanked at the wand, one of his rubber bands snapped. He shoved me, I stumbled against the refreshment table, and the party was over." Beneath the white grease paint, Maxie's mouth turned down in an exaggerated frown. "Being a clown is safe. If I do

103

something klutzy, people just assume it's part of my act."

"Is Leonard Figley the reason you don't like dances?"

"That, and being taller than most guys our age." Embarrassed by the admission, Maxie checked the alarm clock she'd tied to her wrist. "You'd better finish dressing. The guys will be here in half an hour."

Amy scrambled into a pair of electric blue tights and a bright red leotard with glittery stars. The addition of snug knee boots and a foil tiara made her look as though she'd stepped from the pages of a Marvel comic book. "Hey, Clown, toss me my cape, will you?" she requested, slipping on a wide gold bracelet.

Maxie in her oversized shoes flip-flapped to the loveseat. She chuckled as she shook the folds from a length of felt. The words BLUNDER WOMAN were glued to the back of the cape in large, crooked capitals. "I take it John is coming as Captain Fixit," Maxie said.

"What else?" Amy replied.

The door of the suite suddenly swung open to admit an excited, pink-clad alien. Maid Marian was two steps behind.

"Hot off the presses—the latest edition of *The Ledger*," a beaming Shanon informed them, handing Maxie a copy of the newspaper.

The lead story was an account of the shelter children's art exhibit. Maxie's face fell as she studied the photo above the text. It was a picture of her and Jose standing hand-in-hand in front of his painting. Folding the paper, she laid it gently on the desk. "I wish you had waited until after the party to show that to me," she quavered.

"If you cry, you'll ruin your makeup," Palmer scolded. Producing an envelope she had hidden in the folds of her velvet gown, she passed it to Maxie with a smug smile. "Besides, there's no reason for you to be sad anymore."

Maxie did a double-take, then rechecked the handwriting once more for good measure. "It's from Jose!" she finally squealed.

*Dear Max,*

*I thought I was doing you a favor by not writing to you. But Shanon, Amy, and Palmer said you've been very sad.*

Maxie stopped to gape at her suitemates. "What does this mean? Where is Jose? Have you actually seen him?"

"We'll tell you everything later," Shanon said, motioning for Max to continue reading.

*So if it's okay with you, I'd still like to be your pen pal. And this time I promise I'll never, never, never bug out on you again.*

*I've got some good news. I'm going to be able to stay with my family, and one day they're even going to adopt me. My foster dad got a permanent job just outside of Brighton. We're living there in a trailer now, but as soon as he saves enough money, he's buying us a real house. When we get settled, we're going to invite you, Shanon, Palmer, Amy, Mars, John, and Sam to dinner.*

*Oh, yeah. I'm going to school again. I still haven't made any friends there yet, but I have a feeling I will soon.*

*That's about all for now, except that I've really missed you. It feels so grate not to be alone anymore.*

*Your friend,*
*Jose*

105

Maxie put down the letter and turned to her suitemates. "If you don't start talking this very minute," she warned, "I'm going to squirt every one of you with my seltzer bottle."

As the jubilant Foxes supplied a flood of details, Maxie had to swallow hard to hold back tears of happiness. "You guys did all that for me?"

"And for Jose," Shanon said.

"For ourselves, too. We made the mess, so we had to clean it up," Palmer concluded.

Maxie didn't have the words to thank them, so she made the rounds, clasping each of her friends in a bear hug.

"If you get grease paint on my costume, I'll pull your little red nose off," Palmer threatened good-naturedly just as the alarm on Maxie's wrist clock went off.

"Come on, gang—it's show time!" Max said, springing into the air and clicking her heels together.

# CHAPTER 15

John's costume was half Batman, half Superman, and totally hilarious. Executing a heroic leap, he landed beside Amy, improvising, "We can't bob for apples, 'cause we might drown. But our act's going to be the very hottest in town. Captain Fixit—Captain Fixit! Your favorite rapper's here, and we're going to get down!"

"You're a fast-talkin', funny-lookin', left-footed dope. But when the going gets rough, you know how to cope. Blunder Woman—Blunder Woman! She's gonna hog-tie you with her magic rope," she shot back, brandishing her gold-painted lasso.

Her super-hero laughed, squeezing her shoulder affectionately. "I've really missed you. It seems like ages since we last got together."

"Four weeks, two days, sixteen hours, and forty-three seconds—but who's counting?" Amy quipped.

It was always fun being with John. Their relationship was easy, comfortable. And if it were to develop into something a little less comfortable, that would be even better, she suddenly realized. Blushing at the thought, she aimed a playful punch at the backward F pinned to his chest. "Palmer and Georgette want us to do our rap song after the jack-o'-lantern contest. We'd better find a quiet corner and start rehearsing."

"Where's Mars?" Shanon came over to ask. "Didn't he ride over with you, John?"

John shook his head. "Mars is working the Halloween party at the hospital. Just before I left the dorm, he called to say it was running late."

"Oh." There was a world of disappointment packed in the tiny syllable. Swallowing hard, Shanon persisted, "But he *is* coming, isn't he?"

"Of course he's coming," Amy assured her. "Mars would never miss a party. Or a chance to see his pen pal," she added.

"Don't worry, Shanon. If he's not here by ten, Captain Fixit will fly over to Brighton General and drag him back," John promised, flexing his muscles.

Shanon tried to smile at his antics, but her face felt frozen. Intent on hiding her disappointment, she lowered her head—and almost bumped into the dashing, green-clad figure who crossed her path.

"Milady Shanon," he greeted her. "Can you show me the way to Sherwood Forest?" And sweeping off his feathered Robin Hood cap, he bowed grandly.

"Sam O'Leary!" Shanon exclaimed. Her disbelieving gaze swept from his green tights and jerkin to the longbow and arrows strapped to his back. "How come you're not dressed as Marc Anthony?" she asked.

Before he could explain, Palmer floated up to them and

108

Maxie motioned Shanon over to help with the refreshments. As Shanon hurried off, still looking puzzled, Sam turned his admiring gaze on Maid Marian.

"Methinks I see the most fabulous maiden in all of Sherwood Forest," he said, clasping Palmer's hands between his own.

"Methinks you have E.S.P.," Palmer replied, smiling as she tugged at the fringe of his jacket. "This is a neat outfit, but I thought you were coming as Marc Anthony."

"I was—until I heard you were going to be Maid Marian."

"Who told you that?"

"Georgette mentioned it." He scanned the crowd around them, adding, "I'm looking forward to getting to know her better. From the tone of her letter, I'd say she's really a sweet kid."

"She's not half bad, and I—" Palmer stopped in midsentence as Sam's comment suddenly sank in. She stared at him wide-eyed. "Did you just say that my stepsister has been writing to you?"

"Just a note asking me to sing a couple of numbers tonight," he explained. "I thought it was a great idea, but it would've been even better if the invitation had come from you."

"It would have if she wasn't so considerate and unselfish. Palmer didn't want to impose on you," Georgette piped up from behind. She moved between them to slip an arm around Palmer's waist. "Don't you think my big sister's gorgeous, Sam?" she said, batting her big blue eyes at him.

"You bet—and so are you. It's obviously a family characteristic," he responded gallantly.

"Aren't you supposed to be taking care of the music," Palmer reminded her stepsister pointedly.

Georgette's expression changed to concern. "That's why I came over. I didn't mean to interrupt, but there seems to be something wrong with one of the speakers."

"Did you remember to plug it in?" Palmer asked sweetly.

Either the shot went over Georgette's head, or she chose to ignore it. Instead, she turned to Sam and said, "You must be an expert with sound equipment. Would you mind taking a look at it?"

He shrugged. "Sure, but. . . ."

Before he could voice the rest of the objection, Georgette took possession of his arm and dragged him away, calling back over her shoulder, "Kate's looking for you, Palmer. She needs help with the food."

A dull flush of anger rose in Palmer's cheeks. She was about to make a sharp retort when Maxie came bursting over.

"Good news," the clown cried. "Mars has finally arrived. Shanon's in seventh heaven and all is right with the world."

"The heck it is," Palmer growled.

"What's up, Marian? You look kinda hot under the collar," Max observed, playfully aiming her seltzer bottle at Palmer's neck.

"If my beloved stepsister doesn't leave my pen pal alone, I'm going to sink her barge!"

Maxie rolled her gaze to the ceiling, sighing, "I knew it was too good to last."

"Excuse me, Bozo. Are you Max Schloss?" a deep male voice interrupted.

Startled, Max spun around to face the tall, sheet-draped ghost who was standing behind her. In the process, her hand instinctively tightened on the bottle and a stream of seltzer water shot from the nozzle, thoroughly drenching the newcomer.

In spite of her annoyance at Georgette, Palmer couldn't hold back a snort of laughter.

"Sorry about that, Casper," Maxie mumbled as the ghost pulled off the soggy pillowcase that covered his head.

"The name is Paul Grant," he corrected her. "I came with Mars. Actually, I'm crashing the party," he admitted cheerfully, "but he said no one would mind."

Maxie shook the hand he offered, unable to think of a clever reply. Paul Grant looked like a model for a suntan commercial—gold-touched sandy hair, wide shoulders, and a smile that would melt a glacier. His eyes were the exact same green as Max's, and to top it all off, he was a good two inches taller than she was. His grip was firm and confident.

Palmer dug her elbow into Maxie's ribs. "Pull yourself together, Bozo," she whispered.

"Y-you remember Dalmer Purand, don't you?" Maxie blurted.

Paul acknowledged the scrambled introduction with a cordial, "How's it going, Palmer?" but it was clear he was more interested in the clown than Maid Marian.

As Maxie desperately searched for something to say, the soft sounds of a ballad drifted through the air. *Thank goodness*, she thought. Georgette and Sam must have fixed the speaker.

"Want to dance, Max?" Paul asked.

The image of Leonard Figley's face popped into her mind, and she quickly jerked her hand from Paul's. "I can't—I mean—I don't know how."

"That's okay. I can teach you," he offered.

"M-maybe later. I g-gotta go carve a pumpkin," Maxie stammered, backing away. But in her hurry to escape, Maxie's big left clown shoe stumbled over her right one. She would have landed on her rear end if Paul hadn't caught her arm. Embarrassed beyond belief, she pulled away and raced off to the kitchen.

"I guess she doesn't care much for ghosts," Paul said, looking after her wistfully. "I didn't mean to come on too strong, but my roommates think it would be neat if she and I started writing each other," he said. "And I think they've got a good point. I like girls who have a sense of humor—especially when they look like Maxie."

"I need to talk to you, Palmer," Shanon cut in. Throwing a brief "Excuse us" in Paul's direction, she dragged Palmer over to the refreshment table where Amy was waiting.

"That Paul is really adorable. Whatever this is had better be important," Palmer said crossly.

"It is!" Amy practically sang the words. "Check out the ghost who just came in with Mr. Griffith!"

Palmer turned around, now more interested in ghost number two than number one. As the teacher made his way toward the kitchen, his small, sheet-clad companion lagged a step behind. "Either that's the shortest Ardie on record, or it's—"

"Jose!" Amy and Shanon finished in unison.

"This is going to be so good," Palmer squealed. "I can't

wait to see the look on Maxie's face when she sees him," she cried, starting off toward the kitchen.

"We'll hear all the details later," Shanon said, catching her arm. "This moment is for Maxie and her pen pal."

# CHAPTER 16

The previous moment, however, had been all Maxie's. Dashing into the kitchen to escape Paul Grant, she had slipped on a glob of pumpkin seeds someone had dropped. Arms pinwheeling, she'd skidded all the way across the floor before bumping to a stop at the sink. Fortunately, the half-finished jack-o'-lantern on the drainboard was the only witness to her ungainly entrance.

Badly needing an outlet for her frustrations, Max grabbed a knife and began hacking away at the pumpkin. But the grin she carved there seemed scornful, mocking.

"Dumb, stupid, clumsy, gawky, klutzy, jerky dweeb," Maxie scolded herself, underlining each word with an angry jab at the orange fruit. To her mind, the Paul Grant encounter was a hundred times worse than the Figley fiasco. Leonard, after all, had been a ten-year-old nerd who didn't particularly like girls anyway. But Paul was a handsome Ardie who was clearly interested in her. He'd answered her pen pal ad, hadn't he? And even after she'd sprayed him with soda water, he still asked her to dance. The pity of it was that Maxie was interested in him, too. He seemed like a nice guy, and he certainly had a sense of

114

humor. And he was cute!

But there was no way on earth she could ever face him again, she thought, giving the pumpkin a particularly vicious whack. The force of the blow split the jack-o'-lantern in two, sending both halves splattering to the floor.

"What else can happen to me tonight?" Maxie wailed, dropping to her hands and knees to swab at the pulpy mess with a wad of paper towels. This latest in a long line of accidents seemed proof positive that she was hopelessly inept. Wallowing in her misery, she didn't even look up when the kitchen door swung open. "Hi," a muffled voice greeted her.

She turned her head just enough to glimpse a white sheet. Paul! Groaning inwardly, she could only hope that the floor would open up and swallow her whole. "Beat it, Casper. I told you I don't want to dance," she growled, scrubbing so hard her paper towels started to shred.

After a long pause, a hesitant "Me neither" came from under the sheet. It was a male voice, but definitely not Paul's, Max realized. She raised her head for a closer look at the intruder and couldn't help smiling. Unless the seltzer shower had shrunk the tall Ardie considerably, it wasn't Paul's body, either.

Thinking the short visitor might be a child who'd come to the party with one of the faculty members, Maxie rose to her feet and apologized. "I didn't mean to snap," she said. "I got you mixed up with another ghost. Are you looking for your parents?"

"Uh-uh."

Max leaned down to peer into the peepholes cut in the sheet and asked, "Who are you?"

The large dark eyes gave her the answer long before his hesitant "Jose."

115

Maxie felt like doing a headstand, back flip, triple somersault—anything to express the incredible joy that flooded through her. Not only was her pen pal back, he had actually spoken to her! But instinct made her hold her emotions in check. Although Jose had been able to express his thoughts to her in writing, she suspected that dealing with her face-to-face would still be very difficult for him.

"I got your letter today, and I'm so happy that things are working out for you," she said softly. "Would you like to go say hello to my suitemates?"

The head beneath the sheet shook a definite no.

"There's a vampire video playing in the television lounge. Why don't we go check it out?"

Jose nodded and went to retrieve two paper cones of popcorn from the stash of refreshments on the counter.

As the two of them walked hand-in-hand from the kitchen, Maxie felt no need to force a conversation. The trusting clasp of Jose's small fingers said it all.

Much later that night, long after the Foxes had finished a happy rehash of the party's highlights, Max lay staring into the darkness. Slipping from her bed, she tiptoed into the sitting room, sat down at the desk, and began to write.

*Dear Jose,*

*You and I make perfect pen pals because we're very much alike. Both of us have zillions of strange questions whizzing around in our brains, and it isn't always easy to find the answers.*

*For example, I've always wondered about life on other planets, and what it's like to be an octopus. Mostly, though, I'd like to know why I'm such a klutz around boys*

116

*my own age. Playing the clown gets to be a drag, but I don't know how else to act. Maybe you have some suggestions.*

*You don't have to rush right back with the answers, though. We're going to be exchanging letters for a very long time—maybe for the rest of our lives. I may start writing to other pen pals, but you'll always be my numero uno.*

> *Your friend and pen pal,*
> *Maxie*

*P.S. Thanks for taking me to the movie. I know it wasn't a date, but it's probably the closest I'll ever get to one. HA-HA!*

Back in their bedroom, Shanon couldn't sleep either. There was one more thing she had to do, she realized, the final touch that would make her evening complete. Snapping on the lamp, she retrieved her notebook and started to write.

*Dear Lisa,*

*How did you find out that Rob was more than just a pen pal to you? Did a light bulb suddenly click on in your brain? Or did the idea just sneak up on you?*

*I'm asking because tonight, being with Mars felt different somehow. It started when I thought he wasn't coming to the party. I wasn't just disappointed—I was devastated! And when he finally arrived in a goofy, green Martian costume, it felt like Christmas morning and my birthday all rolled into one. He teased me a lot—just like he usually does—but when we started to dance, he held me really*

117

close. There was a special look in his eyes that I've never seen there before.

It scares me to think that our relationship might be different now. You know how much I hate for things to change. But part of me is really excited about it. Growing up isn't easy, is it?

Amy and John were the hit of the party with their "Captain Fixit" rap song. They improvised a couple of verses right on the spot. There was almost a major disaster though. When Sam stepped up to the microphone to sing, Georgette was right by his side. I thought Palmer was going to have a heart attack right on the spot. You know, I can't quite figure Georgette out. She seems so sweet and innocent, but sometimes I think she does things just to needle Palmer. I wonder if Alma Stephens is really big enough for two Durands. Only time will tell, I guess.

One of the best parts of the whole party was Maxie's reunion with her pen pal, Jose. She's a very special person, and Paul Grant was totally impressed with her. To tell the truth, I think they'd make a terrific couple. Amy, Palmer, and I are going to do our best to nudge them together. I hope you'll get to meet Maxie soon, because I think the two of you would really hit it off.

But as much as I like being Max's roommate now, I still miss you tons. Whenever something important happens to me—good or bad—my very first thought is to share it with you. Always remember that I'm here whenever you need to talk. And if things get too tough at home, you can always come back to Alma Stephens. We're all here waiting for you!

Love and kisses,
Shanon

118

**Coming next ... the first ever, bigger, better Pen Pals Super Special!**

In Super Special #1, DREAM HOLIDAY, Palmer, Maxie, Shanon, and Amy head home for Christmas vacation! Palmer can't wait to hit the beach in Florida; Amy's all set to roam the streets of New York; Maxie can't wait to see her rowdy brothers again; and Shanon will get to go to New York for the very first time! Maxie's parents are giving a fabulous holiday party in their Manhattan townhouse, and the Pen Pals are invited! But they don't know the half of it. This could turn out to be the holiday of their dreams! Plus—a chance for you to win a trip to New York to meet your very own pen pal!

**P.S. Have you missed any Pen Pals? Catch up now!**

### PEN PALS #1: BOYS WANTED!

Suitemates Lisa, Shanon, Amy, and Palmer love the Alma Stephens School for Girls. There's only one problem—no boys! So the girls put an ad in the newspaper of the nearby Ardsley Academy for Boys asking for male pen pals.

## PEN PALS #2: TOO CUTE FOR WORDS

Palmer, the rich girl from Florida, has never been one for playing by the rules. So when she wants Amy's pen pal, Simmie, instead of her own, she simply takes him.

## PEN PALS #3: P.S. FORGET IT!

Palmer is out to prove that her pen pal is the best—and her suitemate Lisa's is a jerk. When Lisa receives strange letters and a mysterious prank gift, it looks as if Palmer may be right. But does she have to be so smug about it? Soon it's all-out war in Suite 3-D!

## PEN PALS #4: NO CREEPS NEED APPLY

Palmer takes up tennis so she can play in the Alma-Ardsley tennis tournament with her pen pal, Simmie Randolph III. Lisa helps coach Palmer, and soon Palmer has come so far that they are both proud of her. But when Palmer finds herself playing *against*—not *with*—her super-competitive pen pal, she realizes that winning the game could mean losing *him*!

## PEN PALS #5: SAM THE SHAM

Palmer has a new pen pal. His name is Sam O'Leary, and he seems absolutely perfect! Palmer is walking on air. She can't think or talk about anything but Sam—even when she's supposed to be tutoring Gabby, a third-grader from town, as part of the school's community-service requirement. Palmer thinks it's a drag, until she realizes just how much she means to little Gabby. And just in time, too—she needs something to distract her from her own problems when it appears that there *is* no Sam O'Leary at Ardsley.

## PEN PALS #6: AMY'S SONG

The Alma Stephens School is buzzing with excitement—the girls are going to London! Amy is most excited of all. She and her pen pal John have written a song together, and one of the Ardsley boys has arranged for her to sing it in a London club. It's the chance of a lifetime! But once in London, the girls are constantly supervised, and Amy can't see how she'll ever get away to the club. She and her suitemates plot and scheme to get out from under the watchful eye of their chaperone, but it's harder than they thought it would be. It looks as if Amy will never get her big break!

## PEN PALS #7: HANDLE WITH CARE

Shanon is tired of standing in Lisa's shadow. She wants to be thought of as her own person. So she decides to run for Student Council representative—against Lisa! Lisa not only feels abandoned by her best friend, but by her pen pal, too. While the election seems to be bringing Shanon and Mars closer together, it's definitely driving Lisa and Rob apart.

## PEN PALS #8: SEALED WITH A KISS

When the Ardsley and Alma drama departments join

forces to produce a rock musical, Lisa and Amy audition just for fun. Lisa lands a place in the chorus, but Amy gets a leading role. Lisa can't help feeling a little jealous, especially when her pen pal Rob also gets a leading role—opposite Amy. To make matters worse, the director wants Rob and Amy to kiss!

## PEN PALS #9: STOLEN PEN PALS

Shanon, Lisa, Amy, and Palmer have been very happy with their pen pals—but now they have competition! Four very preppy—and very pretty—girls from Brier Hall have advertised for Ardsley pen pals. And pen pals they get—including Rob, Mars, and John! Soon the boys are living at the rival school as part of an exchange program—and the Fox Hall suitemates' mailboxes are empty. The girls may have had their differences, but there's one thing they can agree on: Brier Hall must be stopped!

## PEN PALS #10: PALMER AT YOUR SERVICE

Palmer's broke! Because of her low grades her parents have cut her allowance. Now she needs to find ways to make money and fast! The Foxes put their heads together to help Palmer with quick money-making schemes *and* to help her with her grades. But they can't do it all. Palmer has to help herself. But will snobby Palmer be able to handle a waitress job?

## PEN PALS # 11: ROOMMATE TROUBLE

Lisa rearranges the suite so that all four girls sleep together in the sitting room. And when shy Muffin Talbot complains that Lorraine Murphy, her new roommate, is a monster, Lisa invites her to sleep in the suite, too. Soon Suite 3-D is so crowded Shanon can hardly study, so she studies in Lorraine's room—and starts to like Lorraine. But her suitemates, especially Lisa, think Lorraine is taking advantage of Shanon.

## PEN PALS # 12: LISA'S SECRET

What's wrong with Lisa? Not even Shanon can find out what's made Lisa change into a grouch overnight. She's irritable, moody, and snaps at everyone. She isn't even cheered up by an invitation to Maggie and Dan's wedding? When the girls hear that Lisa has stopped writing her pen pal, they *know* it's serious. They team up to solve the mystery, but then Lisa announces she's going home, leaving Suite 3-D. But she'll be back . . . right?

## PEN PALS # 13: LISA, WE MISS YOU

Shanon is in for a shock! As Shanon, Palmer, and Amy wait for Lisa to arrive, a tall, red-haired girl walks into Suite 3-D and introduces herself as Max Schloss, their new roommate! Though Max's chauffeur piles more and more luggage into the suite, the girls are convinced there must be some mistake. But is there? What happened to Lisa? And how will Shanon survive a whole school year living with a total stranger?

# WANTED: BOYS — AND GIRLS —
# WHO CAN WRITE !

Join the Pen Pals Exchange and get a pen pal of your own!
Fill out the form below.
Send it with a self-addressed stamped envelope to:

**PEN PALS EXCHANGE**
**c/o The Trumpet Club**
**PO Box 632**
**Holmes, PA 19043**
**U.S.A.**

In a couple of weeks you'll receive the name and address
of someone who wants to be your pen pal.

------------------------------------------------------------------------ Cut here

## PEN PALS EXCHANGE

NAME _____ . GRADE _____

ADDRESS _____

TOWN _____ STATE _____ ZIP _____

DON'T FORGET TO INCLUDE A STAMPED ENVELOPE
WITH YOUR NAME AND ADDRESS ON IT!